AND FIRE POURED FORTH

Alan Baxter

AND FIRE POURED FORTH
6 Tales of Military Horror

From cosmic terrors in underground caverns to warrior nuns protecting humanity to invisible aliens decimating a faraway world, within these pages you'll find six stories of military horror. Taken from the pages of (or inspired by) the SNAFU anthology series, where the remit is for stories crammed with extreme action, monsters, and military mayhem, everything here will leave you breathless.

Lock and load, people. It's going to be intense.

PRAISE FOR ALAN BAXTER

"Alan Baxter is an accomplished storyteller who ably evokes magic and menace." – **Laird Barron**, *author of Swift to Chase*

"Alan Baxter is one of the best horror writers in the business." – **Kealan Patrick Burke**, *Bram Stoker Award-winning author of The Turtle Boy, Kin, and Sour Candy*

"Step into the ring with Alan Baxter, I dare you. He writes with the grace, precision, and swift brutality of a prizefighter." – **Christopher Golden**, *New York Times bestselling author of Ararat and The Pandora Room*

"Alan Baxter delivers a heady mix of magic, monsters and bloody fights to the death. Nobody does kick-ass brutality like Baxter." – **Greig Beck**, *Internationally bestselling author*

"Baxter delivers the horror goods." – **Paul Tremblay**, *author of The Cabin at the End of the World*

"Alan Baxter's fiction is dark, disturbing, hard-hitting and heart-breakingly honest. He reflects on worlds known and unknown with compassion, and demonstrates an almost second-sight into human behaviour." — **Kaaron Warren**, *Shirley Jackson Award-winner and author of The Grief Hole*

"...if Stephen King and Jim Butcher ever had a love child then it would be Alan Baxter." – **Smash Dragons**

"Baxter draws you along a knife's edge of tension from the first page to the last, leaving your heart thumping and sweat on your brow." – **Midwest Book Review**

AND FIRE POURED FORTH
ISBN-13: 978-0-6450019-0-7
13th DRAGON BOOKS

First Trade Paperback Edition – © 2021
Original fiction copyright © 2021 Alan Baxter
Reprinted fiction © Alan Baxter, as listed in Acknowledgements

Cover Design © 2021 Alan Baxter
Internal layout by David Wood

Alan Baxter
www.alanbaxter.com.au

ALSO BY ALAN BAXTER

DEVOURING DARK

HIDDEN CITY

BOUND (Alex Caine Book 1)
OBSIDIAN (Alex Caine Book 2)
ABDUCTION (Alex Caine Book 3)

REALMSHIFT (The Balance Book 1)
MAGESIGN (The Balance Book 2)

SERVED COLD – Short Stories
CROW SHINE – Short Stories

THE GULP
THE ROO
MANIFEST RECALL
RECALL NIGHT
THE BOOK CLUB
GHOST OF THE BLACK: A 'Verse Full of Scum

Co-authored with David Wood

PRIMORDIAL (Sam Aston Investigations Book 1)
OVERLORD (Sam Aston Investigations Book 2)

BLOOD CODEX (Jake Crowley Adventures Book 1)
ANUBIS KEY (Jake Crowley Adventures Book 2)
REVENANT (Jake Crowley Adventures Book 3)

DARK RITE

TABLE OF CONTENTS

FOREWORD

Geoff Brown at Cohesion Press came up with the idea to produce a series of anthologies featuring stories of military horror, where the fundamental requirement was always the same: extreme military (or para-military) action and monsters. Within this over-riding remit, each volume of the ongoing series has a more focussed theme.

I've had the great pleasure of being included in five of these volumes so far: *Survival of the Fittest, Last Stand, Black Ops, Medivac*, and *Future Warfare*. Those five stories are included herein, collected together for the first time. Also included is an original story called "And Fire Poured Forth", which also gives this book its title and adds something never published before to the collection.

The SNAFU anthology series has been wildly successful, and rightly so. It frequently gathers together some of the most amazing writers of horror and action working today, and it's been my pleasure to be included so many times.

The strength of the series is evident not only in its sales and reviews, but also that several of the stories included have been picked up for adaptation to film, in the Netflix series *Love, Death & Robots*, including my own story, "In Vaulted Halls Entombed". That story also won me an Australian Shadows Award and has been translated into German. It's the first story collected here.

I hope you enjoy reading these yarns as much as I enjoyed writing them. And I also hope there'll be many more to come. Lock and load, people. It's going to get intense.

Alan Baxter, NSW Australia, 2021

IN VAULTED HALLS ENTOMBED

Originally published in SNAFU: Survival of the Fittest
This story won the Australian Shadows Paul Haines Award for Long Fiction, and was adapted for film in the Netflix series, Love, Death & Robots.

In Vaulted Halls Entombed

The high, dim caves continued on into blackness.

Sergeant Coulthard paused, shook his heavy, grizzled head. "We're going to lose comms soon. Have you mapped this far?" he asked Dillman.

"Yes, Sarge."

Coulthard looked back the way they had come, where daylight still leaked through to weakly illuminate the squad. "Radio it in, Spencer. See what they say."

"Yes, Sarge." Corporal Spencer shucked his pack and set an antenna, pointing back towards the cave entrance. "Base, this is Team Epsilon. Base, Team Epsilon."

The radio crackled and hissed, then, "Go ahead, Epsilon."

"We've followed the insurgents across open ground to foothills about eighty clicks north north east of Kandahar, to a cave system at... Hang on." Spencer pulled out a map and read aloud a set of co-ordinates. "They've gone to ground, about eighty minutes ahead of us. We'll lose comms if we head deeper in. Orders?"

"Stand by."

The radio crackled again.

"They'll tell us to go in," Sergeant Coulthard said.

Lance Corporal Paul Brown watched from one side, nerves tickling the back of his neck. They were working by the book, but this showed every sign of a trap, perfect for an ambush. It would be dark soon, and was already cold. It would only get colder. Though perhaps the temperature further in remained pretty constant.

He stepped forward. "Sarge, maybe we should set camp here and wait til morning."

"Always night in a fucking cave, Brown," Coulthard said without looking at him.

"You tired, possum?" Private Sam Gladstone asked with a sneer.

The new boy, Beaumont, grinned.

"You always a dick?" Brown said.

"Can it!" Coulthard barked. "We wait for orders."

"I just think everyone's tired," Brown said. He shifted one shoulder to flash the red cross on the side of his pack. "Your welfare is my job after all."

"Noted," Coulthard said.

Silence descended on the six of them. They'd followed this band of extremists for three days, picking up and losing their trail half a dozen times. He was tired even if the others were too hardass to admit it. Young Beaumont was like a puppy, on his first tour and desperate for a fight, but the others should know better. They'd all seen action to some degree. Coulthard more than most, the kind of guy who seemed like he'd been born in the middle of a firefight and come out carrying a weapon.

"Epsilon, this is Base. You're sure this is where the insurgents went?"

"Affirmative. Dillman had them on long range scope. Trying to shake us off, I guess, going to ground."

"Received. Proceed on your own initiative. Take 'em if you can. They've got a lot of our blood on their hands. Can you confirm their numbers?"

"Eight of them, Base."

"Received. Good luck."

Spencer winked at the squad. "Received, Base. Over and out." He unhooked his antenna and slung his pack.

"Okay, then," Dillman said. He shifted grip on his rifle and dug around in his webbing, came up with a night sight and fitted it.

Brown sighed. No one was as good a shot as Dillman, even when he was tired and in the dark. But it didn't give much comfort. "We're not going to wait, are we?" he said.

Coulthard ignored him. "Pick it up, children. As there are no tracks in here," he kicked at the hard stone floor, "we move slow and silent. Spencer, you're mapping. I want markers deployed markers along the way."

"Sarge."

"Let's go. Beaumont, you're on point."

"Yes, Sarge!"

"Slow and steady, Beaumont. And lower that weapon.

No firing until I say so unless you're fired on first."

"Yes, Sarge."

The kid sounded a little deflated and Brown was glad. Youth needed deflating. They fell into order and moved forward. Spencer placed an electronic marker and tapped the tablet he carried. It began to ping a location to help them find their way back.

It became cooler and the darkness almost absolute. The light that leaked through from outside couldn't reach and blackness wrapped them up like an over-zealous lover.

"Night vision will be useless down here," Coulthard said. "We're going to have to risk torchlight. One beam, from point. Dillman, go infrared."

"Way ahead of you," Dillman said, and tapped his goggles. He moved up to stand almost beside Beaumont.

The young private clicked on his helmet lamp and light swept the space as he looked around. The passage was about five metres in an irregular diameter and as dry and cold as everything else they'd seen over the last few days. Dust motes danced in the torch beam, the scuff and crunch of their boots strangely loud in the confined space.

"All quiet from here on," Coulthard said and waved Beaumont forward.

They fell into practised unison, moved with determined caution.

"I'm a glowing target up here," Beaumont whispered nervously.

"That's why the new boy takes point," Coulthard said. A soft wave of giggles passed through the squad before the Sergeant hushed them.

Dillman patted Beaumont on one shoulder. "I got your back, Donkey."

Beaumont's torch beam shot back into the group as he looked around. "Don't call me that!"

Laughter rippled again. Brown grinned. Poor sap. Caught petting a donkey back in Kandahar, just a lonely kid far from home, taking some comfort by hugging the soft, furry creature's neck. Of course, he'd been spotted, photographed and by the time he got back to barracks the story had him balls deep in the poor animal.

"Enough!" Coulthard snapped. "Are we fucking professionals or not?"

Their mirth stilled and they crept forward again. The ground sloped downwards and Spencer paused every fifty yards or so to place a marker. After about three hundred yards the passage opened out into a wider cavern. Something lay rucked up and definitely man-made on the far side.

Weapons instantly trained on it and Beaumont moved cautiously forward. "False alarm," he called back after a moment, his voice relaxed and light. Relieved. "Someone's been here, there are blankets, signs of a fire, an empty canteen. But it looks months old, at least."

The squad relaxed slightly as Beaumont shone his torch in a wide arc, illuminating the cave. Nothing but rough, curved rock. A few small fissures striated the walls on one side, black gaps into the unknown, but nothing big enough for even a child to get through. On the far side, a larger gap yawned darkly, a tunnel leading away and down. Large rocks lay scattered around the opening.

Coulthard nodded the squad forward.

"Looks like these have recently been moved," Gladstone said.

Brown moved in to see better. "Looks like this passage was blocked up and those fuckers cleared the way."

Dillman kicked at a couple of broken stones. "I guess they weren't so keen to ambush us here and are looking for a better option."

Brown shook his head. "Why would this passage have been blocked? And by who?"

"Emergency bolt hole they knew about?" Coulthard mused. "Move on."

The tunnel beyond was around three metres in diameter, sloping down again. Beaumont's was the only light, but in the otherwise total blackness it made the tunnel bright, shadows flickered off the irregular surface.

Beaumont took his flashlight from his helmet and held it at arm's length to one side. "If they do ambush and shoot at the light..."

After a couple of hundred metres, Brown, bringing up the rear, paused and looked back. "Hold up," he said quietly.

Coulthard glanced over his shoulder. "What's up, Doc?"

"Kill the light, Beaumont."

"Gladly!"

There was a soft click and the tunnel sank into blackness. Within seconds, their eyes began to adjust to something other than the dark. In crevices on the walls and ceiling of the passage, even here and there on the floor, a soft blue glow emanated. Almost imperceptible, easier to see from their peripheral vision, a pale luminescence. No, Brown thought. Phosphorescence. He crouched and looked closely into one crack. He pulled out a pocket knife, flicked open the blade and dug inside the crevice. The blade came out with a sickly blue smudge on it.

"Some kind of lichen," he said. "I've heard of this kind of stuff, but always thought it was green."

Gladstone pulled his googles down and flicked the adjustment. "Doesn't matter what colour it is, it's giving enough light for night vision."

"Lucky us," Coulthard said. "Goggles on, people. Keep that light off, Beaumont."

"Thank fuck, Sarge."

Brown pulled his own goggles down and watched the squad move forward in green monochrome. He was glad they didn't need harsh torchlight any more, but the glowing blue lichen gave him the creeps. He stood up and followed before they got too far ahead, shifting his heavy medical pack as he moved.

They continued silently for several minutes, Spencer periodically dropping markers. At a fork they tried the left hand way and quickly met a dead end. Backtracking to the main passage, they travelled further and found a small cave off to one side, too low to stand upright. No passages led from it.

"Looks like this one tunnel is gonna keep heading down," Beaumont said. His voice had lost some of its excitement.

Coulthard raised a fist bringing them to a halt. "How

far?" he asked.

Spencer checked the tablet that shone in their night vision even though its brightness was down to minimum. "Seven hundred and eighty three metres."

"Three quarters of a k in, really?" Dillman whispered.

He sounded as nervous as Brown felt. The strange lichen continued, scattered randomly in cracks and fissures. Occasionally a larger patch would glow like a bright light, but for the most part it was soft streaks like veins in the rocks.

"Move on," Coulthard said.

After another couple of minutes, Spencer whispered, "That's one kilometre."

Before any discussion could be had about that fact, Beaumont hissed and cursed. "Sarge, got something here."

The squad sank into fighting readiness and crept apart to cover the width of the tunnel.

"Bones," Beaumont said. "Just a skeleton."

Coulthard turned. "Doc, go check."

Brown went to Beaumont and looked down on the bones lying at the curve of the tunnel wall. Streaks of the blue lichen wrapped the skeleton here and there, like snail trails. He crouched for a closer look. "Male, adult. No discerning marks of trauma that I can see at first glance."

He took a penlight torch from his pocket and lifted his goggles. "Mind your eyes."

The squad looked away as he clicked on the light and had a closer look. The bones lay scattered, no flesh or connecting tissue remained to hold them together. "There's a kind of residue," Brown said quietly. "Like a gel or something." He took a pen from his pocket and dragged the tip along one femur. It gathered a small wave of clear, viscous ichor. It was odourless.

He put one index finger to the same bone and gently touched the stuff. It seemed inert. As he brought it close to his face to inspect he frowned, then pressed his finger to the bone again. "This is warm."

Tension tightened the squad behind him.

"What's that?" Coulthard asked.

Brown swallowed, heart hammering. He looked at his

fingertip then gripped the bone, felt the heat in his palm. "This skeleton is warm. And too clean to have rotted here."

"What the hell?" Beaumont demanded, his voice quavering.

"You shitting us?" Gladstone asked. His voice was stronger than Beaumont's but with fear still evident.

Brown held one palm over the skeleton, only an inch or so away from touching, moved it back and forth. "It's warm all over," he said weakly. His mind tried to process the information, but kept hitting dead ends. The cold rock under his knee seemed to mock him.

"Warm?" Coulthard asked.

Brown's heart skipped and doubled-timed again as he spotted something beneath the bony corpse. "Hey, Dillman."

"What?"

"When you scoped those fucks we were following, what did you see that you thought was funny?"

A tense silence filled the space for a moment. Then Dillman said, "One of them had a big fucking gold dollar sign on a chain around his neck. Fancied himself a rapper or some shit."

Brown used his pocket knife to hook up a chain from where it hung inside the stark white ribcage. With a toothy clicking, he hauled it up link by link. Eventually a metal dollar sign emerged from between the bones, its surface no longer gold but a tarnished, blackened alloy.

"What the actual fuck?" Beaumont asked in a high voice. He shifted from foot to foot, looked wildly around himself.

"These bones are too clean and white to have decayed to this state," Brown said. He shone his penlight among the bones to show coins, a cigarette lighter, the half-melted remains of a cell phone, belt buckles. Two automatic pistols, both with traces of the gel-like slime, were wedged under the pelvis.

Coulthard stepped forward, leaned down to stare at the corpse like it was a personal insult. "You trying to tell me this is one of the guys we're chasing."

Brown shrugged, hefted the pen to make the dollar sign swing.

"Fuck this," Spencer said. "What the hell can do that to a person?"

Brown shook his head. "Who knows?" He played his torchlight around the walls and ceiling of the tunnel.

"And where did it go?" Gladstone asked weakly.

"Go?" Coulthard asked.

"I think it's pretty clear someone or something did that to him and is no longer here, right?" he said.

"Some kind of weapon?" Beaumont asked, still agitated.

"What kind of weapon does this?" Brown countered.

Coulthard stood up straight. "Can it, all of you. We have a mission and we'll keep to it. We'll find answers on the way."

"It's still warm," Brown reminded him. "This happened very recently, I think."

"Then we move extra fucking carefully," Coulthard said.

A burst of gunfire and distant shouting echoed up the tunnel. Epsilon squad froze and listened. A scream, another burst of gunfire then a deep, concussive boom.

"Grenade?" Dillman asked quietly.

Silence descended again.

"Lights off, mouths shut," Coulthard said. "Brown, up front with me in case we come across any more bodies. Beaumont, rear guard. Move out."

Brown nodded as he pocketed his knife. He wasn't happy about it, but that was a smart move by the Sergeant. Beaumont had sounded very spooked by this encounter and understandably so. His nerves were like an electric current through the squad. Best he go to the back and have a chance to calm down. Reluctantly the squad fell into place. Brown glanced once more at the skeleton on the tunnel floor, and shivered as they moved almost silently away.

They travelled in silence for another ten minutes before Spencer whispered, "Two clicks."

A distant scream rang out, cut off equally fast. Several bursts of gunfire. They froze and listened, but heard nothing more.

"Move on," Coulthard said tightly.

"Are you sure, Sarge?" Brown asked, but the sergeant's only answer was a shove in the back.

Several minutes later, Spencer said, "Three clicks."

Brown pointed and Coulthard nodded. Two more skeletons lay on the tunnel floor. Brown crouched and felt the warmth rising off them, stark against the cold rock all around. Two AK-47s and a variety of other metallic objects littered the ground.

"What the fuck, man?" Beaumont said, his voice still high and stretched. "What can do that?"

"Should we go back?" Brown asked.

"There's still five more of them somewhere ahead," Coulthard said. "And whatever is doing this is ahead as well. We'll go a bit further."

"We gotta go, Sarge!" Beaumont said. "Seriously, how can we fight this fucking…"

"Pull it together, soldier!" Coulthard barked. "Get your shit in order. We go forward for another little while and see. This tunnel has to change at some point, branch off or open out or something. I want to see what happens. If nothing happens by five kays in, we turn around."

"Five kays?" Beaumont sounded like a child. "Fuck man, five kays?"

"Move out," Coulthard said softly, his voice and demeanour a perfect example of calm.

Brown wondered if the Sergeant felt anything like as calm as he acted. It seemed Beaumont was the one having a far more sensible reaction to all this. He bit his teeth together to stem his own trembling and walked on.

The way was still lit by the strange veins of lichen, the tunnel remained a three metre or so diameter throat down into the foothills of the mountain range beyond. They heard nothing more for several minutes.

"Stay alert," Coulthard said. "How you doing, Donkey? Feeling okay?"

Beaumont didn't answer.

The sergeant laughed softly. "Sorry, Josh, I'm only ragging ya. Seriously, you feeling okay? You were a little rattled back there."

No answer.

Sam Gladstone said, "There's no one behind me, Sarge."

"What?"

"He was bringing up the rear, but he's not there."

Coulthard spat a curse. "Beaumont!" he called out in a harsh whisper. "Fuck, surely he hasn't panicked and run back."

"Wouldn't I have heard, Sarge?" Gladstone asked.

"I don't know. Would you? Spencer, leave your tablet here and double time back up the tunnel. If you don't catch up to him in a few hundred yards, we'll have to let him go and I'll kick his fucking ass when we get back."

"Righto, Sarge."

Spencer put down his gear and jogged away. They stood in uncomfortable silence for a few minutes.

"Nervous kid," Brown said eventually. "First tour."

"Don't make excuses for him," Coulthard said. "He's a fucking soldier."

Spencer walked back towards them, holding something out. "We need to get the fuck out of here," he said. Hanging from his fingers was a chain with two dog tags.

"The fuck?" Dillman whispered.

"Beaumont's?" Coulthard asked in a tight voice.

"He's a fucking skeleton just like the insurgent fuckers we found. Nothing left but buckles and weapons and shit. He's just fucking bones, Sarge!"

Dillman began muttering and shone his helmet lamp frantically in every direction. The mood of the squad began to fracture.

Coulthard swatted Dillman's lamp off. "Stow that shit! Everyone stay calm."

"Calm, Sarge?" Gladstone asked. "Seriously, we're in deep shit here."

"Stay. Calm. Spencer, did you recover Beaumont's weapon."

Spencer shook his head. "Left it there. The strap is gone, too hard to carry. But I took his clips."

"Fair enough. Now, we need to reassess what we're doing here."

"I think we should leave, Sarge," Brown said. He tried to keep his voice calm, but heard and felt the quaver in it.

"It ain't that simple."

"It must be," Dillman said. "Fuck those guys, if they're even still alive down there. Whatever got Beaumont can get them. We'll wait outside the caves and pick off any who come out."

Coulthard held up a hand, a pale green wave in their night vision goggles. "Chill, everyone. It ain't as simple as leaving. I'm with you, in any other circumstances I would absolutely call an abort. But whatever took Beaumont, it took him from the back."

"Which means it's behind us," Brown said, realisation like an icy wave through his gut. "Or there's more than one, ahead and behind."

"Exactly."

"Does that mean we should carry on though?" Gladstone asked. "Maybe it's only gonna get worse."

"Maybe. Or maybe there's another way out." Coulthard picked up Spencer's tablet, checked the display. "We've still got a bunch of sensors, yeah?"

Spencer dropped Beaumont's tags into a pocket. "Yeah, plenty."

"Okay. We carry on for another kilometre and see if it leads to any branches in the tunnel, any other way out. If it does, we can maybe go around whatever's in here. If not, we turn around and risk facing it. Spencer, it's unlikely but do we have any signal down here?"

The Corporal pulled out his gear and spent a moment trying to get a response from Base. Then he went wide band, looking for any transmissions. He found none and no one responded to open hails. "Nothing, Sarge."

"I didn't think so. Okay, Brown, you stay in the middle. Me and Spencer will take point. I want Gladstone and Dillman on rear guard, but you two walk backwards. We move slow and you don't take your eyes off the tunnel behind us. Let's go."

They moved slowly on again. Brown felt more than a little useless in the middle of the group, but he knew what Coulthard was doing. Protect the guy with the best chance of helping any wounded. Except it looked like whatever was in these caves didn't leave any wounded. He heard a gasp from Gladstone and turned to look.

"See that?" Gladstone whispered to Dillman.

"Yeah. There!"

Brown saw it too. He lifted his goggles to see with unfiltered eyes. A movement, more a shift of light across the darkness, like a ripple of wan blue luminescence. He caught part of a smooth, glassy sphere, a glimpse of something globular, but it pressed into the wall and vanished.

The others had stopped to watch. All five of them stared hard, but the tunnel was black as death and still.

"Keep moving," Coulthard said.

Brown walked backwards as well, eyes trying to scan every inch of the tunnel behind them.

"There!" Gladstone said sharply.

He'd seen it too. A glassy flex of movement on the ceiling about thirty metres back, closer than before. Almost as if a giant water droplet had begun to swell and hang, only to be quickly sucked back up.

"It's fucking following us," Dillman hissed and snapped on his helmet light again.

"But what is it?" Spencer demanded. "Is it even alive? Doc?"

Brown jumped as he was directly addressed. "I'm no expert here," he said. "Whatever it is…"

His words were drowned out by Gladstone's screams and Dillman's shouts of fright as the torchlight reflected back off a huge slithering mass across the ceiling right above them. It ran and undulated like an upside down river across the rock then expanded, long and pendulous, extruding from the tunnel roof like a clear jelly waterfall. The huge, gelatinous blob unfurled itself and dropped.

Dillman leapt to one side, the deafening bark and muzzle flash of his weapon filling the tunnel as Gladstone tried to run backwards, but skidded and fell. He knocked Brown back, who dropped onto his rump in surprise and scrambled away, scrabbling for his weapon as Coulthard and Spencer aimed theirs above his head and let rip.

Gladstone's screams were bloodcurdling as the thing

landed across his legs. Brown tried to see through the bursts of muzzle fire and caught staccato images like through a strobe light. Gladstone's legs, clothing and flesh alike, melted away inside the transparent blob in an instant, leaving only bones. He tried to batter it off with his hands only to raise fleshless, stark white fingerbones in horror that fell and scattered across his lap. The meat of his arms was gone to his elbows in a second. Tenticular appendages lashed forward from the globular mass and retracted like a frantic sea anemone as it filled the tunnel with its bulk. Hails of bullets from Dillman, Spencer and Coulthard slapped and sputtered into the thing with little effect. It seemed to flinch and flex away from the bullets, then surge forward again, relentless. Only Dillman's torch beam seemed to really hold it up. Gladstone's screams cut abruptly short as it reached his torso and then Brown was up and running.

He pounded down the tunnel and realised the others were with him. At least, Spencer and Coulthard were. They panted as they ran, intent only on putting distance between themselves and that fetid horror. He didn't dare look back for fear the thing was bulging along behind them, for fear he'd see Gladstone finished off or Dillman caught. He stumbled and nearly fell sprawling at one point as the tunnel floor became broken rock and one wall half-fallen, almost blocking the way. The result of the grenade they had heard earlier. Bones scattered as he kicked unwittingly through another skeleton.

A brighter glow began to fill the tunnel ahead and he pounded for it, heedless to any danger before them compared to the certain death behind.

They burst out into a dizzyingly huge cavern, skidding to a halt on a rock ledge that protruded into space hundreds of metres above the cave floor. The ceiling was lost in swirling mists far above, but a soft blue glow leaked through. The walls of the gigantic space were streaked with the strange lichen and the entire place swam in a surreal glow, almost like wan daylight leaking through tropical waters, incongruous several kilometres underground. Filling the floor and rising high into the wisps of mist was a structure clearly constructed by intelligent design, a huge spiralling tower, hundreds of metres high, with a base at least a kilometre across. Curving buttresses met smaller towers in a circle around it. Monumental, the organic-looking structure appeared to have been painstakingly carved from the rock itself. From their ledge, a mammoth stairway led down to the building's lowest levels and the cave floor. Each stair was around two metres high and a similar width, hundreds of the giant steps leading down into haze. The air was colder and damp, smelled metallic and ancient. Everything about the sight emanated age, beyond any span of history. Geological age.

"Fuck me," Spencer said, lifting his goggles. His voice held the taint of madness.

They jumped and spun at a scuffing, puffing sound from behind. Dillman staggered from the tunnel mouth, moaning in agony. His left arm was nothing but useless, dangling bone, his hand gone. Half his face was missing, teeth grinning from the exposed skull where the bubbling, bleeding skin still retracted. "Saaarrrge," he slurred, reaching out with his good hand as he fell to one knee.

Spencer staggered backwards and turned, vomited noisily. Brown hurried forward, his medical training taking over, pushing shock and horror aside for the moment. But he didn't dare touch the poor bastard. He looked closely, trying to ascertain where the damage ended. Dillman's shoulder was eaten away and still melting. The cartilage holding the whole joint together disintegrated as Brown watched and Dillman's arm bones fell to the rock with a clatter. The flesh of his neck liquefied and blood pulsed from the exposed carotid artery.

Dillman scrabbled at Brown one-handed as the medic gaped, at a total loss, even as the creep of disintegration slowed to a stop. But the damage was irreversibly done and Dillman's lifeblood pumped out. Coulthard's barrel slid into Brown's vision, pressed up against Dillman's forehead, and barked. The poor bastard flew backwards as the back of his head exploded out across the cave wall.

Spencer continued to empty the contents of his stomach

as Brown sank to his knees and shook, mind flatlining. Coulthard moved to the mouth of the tunnel they'd emerged from and stared into the darkness. He flicked on his helmet torch and the beam pierced the black. He played it over the walls and ceiling.

As Spencer finally stopped puking, gasping short, shuddering breaths, Coulthard said, "Doesn't seem to be following us. Maybe it just guards the tunnels."

"Guards?" Brown managed.

Coulthard gestured at the impossible subterranean structure. "I don't think anyone is supposed to find that, do you?"

"But what is it?" Brown asked. "What manner of creature..?"

"Best not try to figure it out," Coulthard said. "Ours are soldier minds. That kind of question is for scientists."

"I can't believe it didn't get all of us," Spencer said.

"Out of practice maybe," Brown wondered. "It's not that quick, for all its deadliness. We only saw four insurgent bodies too. So four more got past it. It didn't like our lights, though they only slowed it."

"The flashlights were more use than the gunfire," Spencer said.

"Maybe too bright out here," Coulthard said, staring out into the wan blue glow of the cavern.

"Look."

Coulthard and Brown turned to see where Spencer pointed. Several giant staircases like the one in front of them led from the cavern floor up to various ledges around the walls. Their ledge covered a hundred metres with another staircase leading down from the far end. On that stairway, four tiny figures were clambering resolutely down. They moved as if exhausted, sitting on the edge of each high step before slipping onto the one below. One of them was being helped by the others, clearly wounded.

"Fuckers," Coulthard said. He went to Dillman's corpse, unslung the man's sniper rifle and fitted a telescopic sight. Moving to the edge of their own top stair he dropped onto his belly and unfolded the supports beneath the rifle's barrel to aim across and down.

"Seriously, Sarge?" Brown asked, incredulous.

"We have a fucking job to do, gentlemen. I'll see that done properly, at least."

He squeezed the trigger and one insurgent's head burst with a spray of blood they could see from afar, even with the naked eye. The others became frantic, scrambling like frightened ants. Coulthard fired again and a second man went down as his chest burst open. Another shot and the wounded insurgent was hit in the shoulder and spun around to drop to the rock and crawl into the lee of a huge step out of sight. They had finally realised where the fire was coming from and the other man scrambled into cover as well.

"Fuckers," Coulthard said again. He kept his eye to the sight and lay still, breathing gently.

Spencer sank to curl up against the wall at the back of the rock shelf. His arms wrapped around his head and he rocked gently.

"Spencer's lost it," Brown whispered to Coulthard.

"I know," the Sergeant said without taking his eye away from the telescopic sight. "Give him some time and see if he comes around."

"How much time do we have?"

"Who knows? Right now, that fucking thing isn't coming out of the tunnel and I'm certainly not going back in. There's one unhurt insurgent bastard down there and one with a shoulder wound of unknown severity. For now, I plan to wait them out and give Spencer a chance to get his shit together. I suggest you have a rest."

His tone brooked no further discussion. Brown moved well away from the tunnel mouth and sat down against the stone. It was cold on his back. Clearly Coulthard had lost it too, only he was dealing with it in a typically old school military way. The big, musclebound sergeant had seen more action than the rest of them put together and he let all that training take over. Maybe it was a good strategy. If the man could divorce himself from his emotions and let his experience run him like a robot, perhaps that would actually see him out of this alive.

Time ticked by. Brown began to worry about more mundane matters like where they might sleep, how much they had left in the way of rations and water, whether there was any way out other than the way they had come in. And he certainly wasn't keen to go back up the tunnel either.

He jumped as Coulthard's rifle boomed.

"I knew I could outwait him," the sergeant said with a smile in his voice.

"Did you get him?"

"Yep. He didn't think I'd wait on a scope all that time. I've sat for longer than ten minutes, you murderous insurgent motherfucker. You're a fucking amateur, you had to peek. A dead fucking amateur now." He stood and slung the rifle over his shoulder. "All dead except the shoulder wound and I reckon he'll bleed out if nothing else. Let's go and see."

Brown stood, brow knitted in confusion. "Go and see?"

"Yep. What else is there to do?"

Brown thought hard but came up empty. The Sergeant had a point. They at least needed to look around if they didn't plan to go back up the tunnel they had entered by, so they might as well finish the job while they searched. It was pragmatism taken to the max, but it made a cold sense.

Coulthard went and crouched beside Spencer. "How you doing, soldier?"

"Not good, Sarge."

"Me either. But we gotta move, okay?"

Spencer looked up, his narrow face white as bone under his brown crewcut. "I got a little boy at home, Sarge. He's gonna be two next month. I'm due home in time for his birthday. I missed his first."

Coulthard patted Spencer's shoulder. "We'll get out and get you on a transport home just when you're supposed to be."

"We won't, Sarge. None of us are getting out." He pointed at the spires and tower filling the cavern. "What the fuck even is that, Sarge? We're gonna die here." He sounded perfectly calm about it.

"We're getting out," Coulthard said firmly.

"My wife always worried I'd come home with no legs

from an IED. 'You won't get killed,' she said one night when we'd been drinking. 'I can feel that.' She was always what she called spiritual. Thought she was fucking psychic, you know? But it was harmless. 'You won't get killed,' she said, 'but I have a terrible feeling you're going to be maimed by a mine.' Great fucking prophecy, eh, Sarge? For all her spirituality, she certainly didn't foresee this shit!"

Coulthard laughed. "I don't think anyone foresaw this shit."

"I was supposed to go home in two weeks, Sarge." Spencer's eyes brimmed with tears.

Brown gaped as Coulthard did something he would never have anticipated. The Sergeant gathered Spencer into a tight hug and held the man against his chest.

"Let it out, solider," Coulthard said, and Spencer sobbed.

Brown stood uncomfortably off to one side for a good minute while Spencer bawled. The medic wondered why he felt so calm, so cold inside, and realised he had his terror, his panic, locked up in his chest. His true self and all the emotions it harboured was in a sealed box inside him and at some point he would have to unlock that box. It frightened him to think what might happen when he did, but for now, it stopped him falling to pieces. Did that make him a better soldier than Spencer? A worse human being? For all the atrocities he'd seen, all the wounds and trauma he'd become accustomed to, surely this day's experiences should break him. He had no wife or kids like Spencer to yearn for. But the Sergeant did and he was holding it together too. Maybe Spencer had just lost control of his locked box for now.

Coulthard pushed the man away. "Right, now on your feet, son. Feel better."

"Sorry, Sarge, I just..."

"Fuck sorry, Spencer, it's all done. You ready to move out?"

"Yes, Sarge." Spencer's voice still quavered, but there was some confidence back in it.

"Brown?"

The medic nodded, shook himself. "Yes, Sarge." *At least*, he thought, *as ready as I possibly can be.*

Coulthard sniffed and settled his pack. "Well, I am certainly not going back the way we came. That thing in the tunnel, whatever it is, seems to want to stay there, so we'll leave it well alone. There must be another way out. Nothing that size," he pointed at the monumental structure filling the cave, "can possibly only have one tiny tunnel leading in. Let's go."

"Sarge," Brown said, finally ready to give voice to a nagging worry that had tickled his hindbrain since they had emerged onto the rocky ledge.

"What?"

"The thing in the tunnel hasn't followed us out. Maybe you're right and it's too bright in here."

"Yeah. And?"

"Well, if it's meant to guard this place, but hasn't followed us out, that must mean something."

The Sergeant narrowed his eyes. "Like maybe there's something else in here to do the same job and that thing only worries about its tunnel?"

"Something like that."

"You have a point. Better keep your weapon ready. Let's go."

They moved along the ledge, heading for the giant stairway leading down that the insurgents had used. Brown whistled softly as they came abreast of a massive bronze plate pressed into the wall, ten metres high and five wide, inscribed with strange cursive symbols and patterns that made him dizzy to look upon. His eyes kept sliding away as he tried to make sense of them and nausea began to stir his guts.

"Over there," Spencer said. "And there."

They followed his pointing finger and saw other plaques on other ledges dotted around the cave. Small tunnel openings here and there accompanied them just like the one they had entered through.

"Any of those tunnels could have a fucking monster like the one that attacked us," Brown said.

"We have to assume each one does," Coulthard said. "We have to keep looking for something else. Move on."

Another twenty metres along their ledge gave them a vantage point past the monumental structure and they all saw it at once. On the far side of the vast cave, at the top of another giant staircase that went even higher than where they currently stood, a huge tunnel mouth yawned open.

"That must be fifty metres wide," Coulthard said. "We have a fighting chance in a space like that."

"Probably where the insurgents were heading too," Brown said. "Means going through that structure though."

"Or around it on ground level."

A scream ripped through the air. High pitched and horrified, it was the voice of a man staring into hideous death and it cut suddenly short.

"Came from down there." Spencer pointed down the stairway they had nearly reached, where the insurgents had died under Coulthard's fire.

"Seems like old Shoulder Wound survived after all," the sergeant said.

"Until just then." Brown felt the lock on the box in his chest loosening.

"Alright. Silence." Coulthard raised his weapon and headed for the stairs. "We have no choice but to go through, so let's *fight* our way through."

He moved to the first stair and jumped down. The riser was a few inches above his head, but he walked forward and jumped down the next. Brown and Spencer followed.

Brown's knees jarred with every drop and he wondered how long they would hold out. How long could any of them last with this kind of exertion? The insurgents were about two thirds of the way down and had looked spent, sliding off each step, staggering around.

And assuming they made it down, they would have to climb up even more stairs to get to the wide tunnel they had seen. And all the while fighting past whatever had triggered that scream? Basic training or advanced combatives, nothing prepared a soldier for this. Ready for anything? No one had ever listed this place under the heading of "anything".

His lock loosened a little more, so Brown stopped thinking and kept moving.

He stopped counting the drops at fifty, but after a few more Coulthard paused and raised one fist. They froze, crouched in readiness. Coulthard tapped his ear. Straining to listen, Brown heard a scratching, scrabbling noise. Distant, but getting quickly nearer. Coulthard crept to the edge of the step they were on to look down and immediately burst into action. He raked his assault rifle left to right, the reports of his short bursts shattering the quiet and bouncing back from the distant walls all around. Brown and Spencer joined him at the edge. Spencer added his ordnance to Coulthard's straight away, but Brown paused momentarily, stunned.

A flood of creatures flowed up the steps towards them like roiling black water. Only twenty or so steps below and fast getting closer, they scrambled on too many legs, black bodies like scorpions, but where the stinger should be on the end of the waving tails was a leering face, almost human though twisted somehow into something hideously uncanny, eyes too wide, mouths too deep. Those mouths stretched silently open or gaped like fish as the creatures chittered over the stone edges. Each was a metre or more long, two vicious mandibles at the front of the thorax snapping at the air as they came.

Brown brought his weapon up and added his fire to the fray. Their bullets tore into the things, shattering hard shells and causing gouts of glowing blue blood. As one fell, its fellows swarmed over it. Some staggered from shots striking their many limbs and fell from the sides of the staircase. Brown realised the things were screaming, in fear or pain or triumph he didn't know, but they had no voice and just hissed thick streams of air from those stretched and awful faces that wavered atop their segmented tails as they ran.

There was no way Brown and his colleagues would be able to scramble up the stairs ahead of these horrors, so here they had to make their stand. Coulthard plucked a grenade from his belt and lobbed it past the first wave. It detonated in a cloud of shining black carapace and stone chunks. Spencer emptied his clip and expertly switched in a new one. He resumed firing as Brown switched in new ammo. Coulthard threw two more grenades and switched clips to resume firing. Brown threw a grenade of his own and switched in his last clip. Their automatic fire stuttered and roared, controlled bursts as training took over.

The creatures were only five steps away, then four, and ammo was running out. Brown, Spencer and Coulthard yelled incoherent defiance and raked fire across their advance. Spencer lobbed a grenade then the things were too close for any more explosives.

Three steps and their numbers finally began to thin, two steps, almost close enough to touch.

Suddenly the men were stumbling left and right, firing in short bursts as the last of the things breached their step and tried to clamber onto them, heavy, sharp mandibles snapping rapidly for limbs. Spencer screamed as one drew close, his weapon clicking absurdly loudly, empty. Brown fired three short bursts and then there were no more creatures coming. Coulthard blew two away right at his feet, turned and killed the last one right before it leapt onto Spencer.

Everything was suddenly still, their ears rang.

Dave Spencer looked up at his sergeant with a smile of relief just as Brown raised one hand and shouted, "Stop!"

But Spencer finished taking a step away from the corpse at his feet and his foot vanished over the edge of the stairway. As his face opened into an O of utter surprise, he dropped from sight.

Brown and Coulthard rushed to the edge, but Spencer was lost in shadow. He found his voice a second later, his howl drifting up before cutting off with a wet thud. Silence descended heavily throughout the enormous cavern.

Brown, on his hands and knees, began to tremble uncontrollably. "So much for his psychic fucking wife," he muttered.

Coulthard was beside him, breathing heavily from exertion, as Brown was, but there was anger in the sergeant's demeanour too. "Took the fucking radio with him," Coulthard said eventually.

He stood and yelled and screamed, kicked at the corpses of the horrible scorpion monsters all around. Brown turned to sit and watch, glad in a way that the man was finally letting some emotion out. Like a pressure cooker, he had surely been close to blowing for a long time.

Eventually the sergeant slumped back against the step above and slid down to sit. "So all we have is what we're carrying and no comms."

Brown nodded. "I've got what's left in here," he hefted his weapon, "and that's it. You?"

"Same."

"I still have two grenades."

"I got none. But we each have pistols," Coulthard said.

"Might save that for myself," Brown said quietly, and he meant it. At some point, sticking the barrel of the .45 against his temple and pulling the trigger seemed like a good option. He looked at the chitinous corpses all around. "Think we got them all?"

"Hope so. These ancient fuckers were no match for the tools of modern warfare."

"Tools which will be empty very soon if we need to use them again."

Coulthard just nodded, staring at the ground between his feet. Eventually he sniffed decisively, stood. "Right, let's go."

Brown looked up at him, stark against the backdrop of shadowy mist and the wan blue glow of the lichen. "Yeah. Okay."

They began to drop down the steps again, picking their way through the broken bodies, blue blood and shattered rock of their battle. In places, their grenades had sheered the steps into gravel slides they carefully surfed on their butts. Here and there some of the creatures still twitched, but they avoided them and preserved their ammo. After a dozen or so stairs the corpses ended. Another couple and they came across red smears on the stones and a few lumps of flesh and ragged clothing.

"A lot of blood," Brown noted. "Those things clearly enjoyed the dead as well as the one who survived. I sure hope that was all of them we killed."

Coulthard nodded and continued down in silence.

Eventually, gasping, with legs like jelly and bruised feet, they reached the bottom to stand in swirls of mist.

A low moan rose, vibrating the air all around them. The stone floor thrummed. Then it faded away. As Brown and Coulthard turned to look at each other, it rose again, louder, stronger. Then again. And again. Each time, it vibrated more deeply, sounding more strained and desperate, accompanied by a heavy metallic clattering. Then silence fell and pressed in on them for a long time.

Eventually Brown said, "What the fuck was that?"

Coulthard looked towards the tall structure in the centre of the cave. From ground level it punched up high above them, wreathed in tendrils of blue-tinged mist. Brown began to dizzy as he stared up at it. The smaller towers surrounding the base, connected with curving buttresses, were each some thirty metres high. In the base of each smaller tower was a hollowed out circular space and in that space sat a statue. From the few he could see, Brown realised that each statue was turned to face the centre tower. They were almost human-like in form, seated cross-legged, but each had four arms with eight-fingered hands, held out to either side as though awaiting an embrace. Their bellies were distended and rolled with fat, their faces wide with four eyes, two above two. Brown moved to better examine the nearest one and the level of detail was phenomenal, disturbing. Not so much carved, as real living things turned instantly to stone. He wondered if in fact that's exactly what they were. Each was at least three metres tall and corpulent.

Coulthard's gaze was still fixed on the main tower. Brown moved to stand beside him and realised he was looking at a doorway, a dark opening in the rock wall several metres high and a couple wide. "The moaning came from inside, don't you think?" the sergeant asked.

"Who cares?" Brown said, stunned.

"I have to know." Coulthard walked towards the door.

"Sarge? Seriously, let's just go. What if more of those..." Brown's voice trailed off as Coulthard approached the opening.

Soft blue light pulsed from inside as the sergeant drew

near. The moan rose again, shaking everything. Brown put a hand to his chest as the deep moan sounded a second time and made his heart stutter. His feet were frozen to the spot as he watched Coulthard step through the high entrance.

The sergeant stopped just inside and his gaze rose slowly upwards. He was framed in the blue light, that pulsed more and more rapidly. The groaning became a wail and Coulthard's weapon dropped from lax fingers to hang by its shoulder strap. "Chains," Coulthard stammered. He looked left and right, up and down, his sight exploring a vast area. "Giant chains right through its flesh. Through all those eyes!" He dropped to his knees, head tilted back as he looked far above himself. "This is a prison. An eternal prison!" He began to laugh, a high, broken sound that came from the root of no sound mind.

The moan stirred into a deep, encompassing voice that reverberated through the cavern. "*Release me!*"

Chains rang as they were snapped taut and relaxed again. Whatever slumbering monstrosity that filled the tower and split the edges of Coulthard's mind thrashed and its voice boomed again. "*RELEASE ME!*"

"Sarge!" Brown yelled, his stomach curdled with terror. "We have to go!"

He wanted to drag his sergeant away, but had no desire to risk seeing what the man saw. "*Sarge!*" he screamed.

Coulthard's face tipped slightly towards him and Brown took in the sagging cheeks, drooling mouth, wild, glassy eyes, and knew that Coulthard was lost. No humanity remained in that shell of a body. With a sob, Brown ran.

He raced around the tower and leaped for the first step of the stairway on the far side. He hauled himself up as the voice burst out, over and over, "*Release me! Release me! Release me!*"

Brown scrambled up stair after stair, rubbing his hands raw on the rough surface. He sobbed and gasped, his shoulder and back muscles burned, but he hauled on and on. He couldn't shake the image of all those swarming scorpion things from his mind and imagined them racing up behind him, but didn't dare to look. The voice of whatever was imprisoned below cried out again and again.

At some point, more than fifty steps up, Brown collapsed, exhausted, and blackness took over. He assumed he was dying and let himself go.

He had no idea how much time had passed when he woke again, unmolested. The massive cavern was still.

Brown dragged himself to his feet and began the shattering climb once more, step after step after step. Time blurred, his mind was an empty darkness, until he pulled himself over the top of one more step and saw a flat expanse of rock stretching out before him. On the far side, some hundred metres away, the huge yawning tunnel stood, threatening to suck him in.

Brown laughed, dangerously close to hysterical, and gained his feet, stumbled forward into the gloom. He didn't care what might be there, he just needed to leave the hideous monument and its prisoner behind.

More of the softly glowing lichen striated the walls and he dropped his night vision goggles into place. The sight before him stopped him dead, confused. A grid, some kind of lattice. He looked up and down as realisation dawned. A giant portcullis-like gate filled the tunnel, thirty metres high, fifty metres across, fixed deeply into the rock. He walked up to it and found it made of cast metal like the huge plaques they had seen, the criss-crossed straps of bronze at least twenty centimetres thick. Each square hole of the lattice was perhaps half a metre or a little more across. If he stripped off his gear, he might be able to squeeze through. Or he might very well get stuck halfway.

But it didn't matter. Beyond the gate, beyond the weak glow of the cavern behind him, uncountable numbers of clear, globular shapes moved and writhed, tentacles gently questing out and retracting again, waiting, hungry. Hundreds of them.

Brown fell to his butt and sat laughing softly. He checked his rations and canteen, tried to estimate how long he might survive, and gave up when his brain refused to cooperate. He looked back across towards the tunnel they had emerged from. Compared to the swarm waiting beyond the gate, the one or two in that tunnel seemed like far better odds. Assuming it was only one or two. And assuming he had the strength to get back down and up again. And that there were no more guardians waiting for him in the cavern. And that whatever was imprisoned below didn't thrash free in its rage.

Lance Corporal Paul Brown, experienced medic and decorated solider, lay down and pulled his knees up to his chest. His brain couldn't work out what to do, so perhaps he would just have a sleep and, refreshed, maybe then decide which suicidal option for escape might be the best one to try.

SPECIAL COMMUNIQUE.
ATTN: COLONEL ADAM LEONARD – DIRECTOR, UNEXPLAINED OCCURRENCE DIVISION.
YOUR EYES ONLY
SUBJECT – DISAPPEARANCE OF EPSILON TEAM, NORTH OF KANDAHAR, AFTER TRACKING ENEMY INSURGENTS TO UNDERGROUND HIDEOUT.
SURVIVORS – 1: LANCE CORPORAL PAUL BROWN, MEDIC.
REPORT: After non-response from Epsilon Team for thirty six (36) hours after their last communique, a second squad was sent to investigate. They found Lance Corporal Paul Brown of Epsilon stumbling through foothills some seven (7) kilometres south of Epsilon Team's last known whereabouts. Brown was wearing nothing but ragged underwear and his helmet, raving and largely incoherent, his left arm below the elbow was just bone, no hand, the flesh stripped away presumably by acid or a similar agent. His body was covered in various other

wounds, some similar to his arm (though none as severe) and others clearly made from impacts, falls, scrapes, etc. He carried no gear except a flashlight, which he pointedly refused to relinquish. He made almost no sense except one phrase, repeated over and over: "Never let it out! Never let it out!" Current assessment by psychologists suggests Brown may never recover his faculties, but therapy has been started. His extensive injuries are being treated and are responding satisfactorily.

We're still trying to establish further facts but are preparing an incursion squad to Epsilon's last known whereabouts. Due to your standing request to be informed of any unusual occurrences, I am sending this wire. Our squad will be entering the cave at the last known location of Epsilon Team at 0800 tomorrow, the 14th, should you wish to accompany them.

Please advise.

RAVEN'S FIRST FLIGHT

Originally published in SNAFU: Black Ops, this story was a finalist for the 2016 Aurealis Award for Best Fantasy Novella.

Raven's First Flight

Raven sat on a hard metal chair and scanned the bare room. A huge mirror on one wall was obviously a one-way window. Otherwise there were two chairs and a square metal table, all bolted in place. The room itself lay buried deep in an otherwise normal office complex, on the top floor of an old brownstone on East 72nd Street on the Upper East Side of Manhattan. An office like a million others across New York. She thought she'd already agreed to join this strange crew, despite the lack of details, but it felt like another interview was imminent. Or maybe she'd misread everything and was being taken for a ride.

Raven. She liked the new handle. She'd never really liked her given name anyway. *Real identity no longer exists in the Dark Squad*, she had been told. *No names, no history, no family, your new life starts here and before that you were nothing. The old you is a ghost.*

It suited her fine. Being rid of her loser parents would be no trauma, she'd left them for the Army at sixteen, first chance she got. And they'd left the rest of her family behind in Korea anyway. She hadn't seen any of *them* since she was five. Growing up Korean in America, a cultural mongrel, nothing had come easily to her. Estranged not only by distance and emotional coldness, but by her powers too, the odds had always been against much in the way of integration. Which was apparently a large part of why she'd been picked for this weirdo sideline. She was yet to decide if she could really trust the promises that had been made to her, but anything appealed more than a cell. A slight guilt hovered at the thought of her parents receiving a 'Killed In Action' notice, the funeral without a body they would have to endure. But still, what did she really care?

A light burst out, blinding her. Raven ducked off the chair, rolled into a crouch by the furthest wall, standard procedure against an unexpected IED. Her Army training fired up and she slipped the automatic 9mm from its hip holster, squinted against the blur as her vision adjusted back to normal. Nothing to shoot at, no burn or explosive damage. A decoy blast? She switched the 9mm to her left hand, trained on where the light had seemed to emanate, and moved her right hand to the jade knife at her belt, slipped it free. Its icy touch emboldened her. Feeling suitably armed, she whispered the *samjok-o* into her presence. The three-legged raven, it's jet black feathers glistening under harsh blue strip lighting, stepped as though through an unseen door directly onto her shoulder.

What's here? Raven mentally whispered to the familiar, the source of her new operative name.

It ducked and blinked, hopped up and circled the room with one wing flap, then settled back to her shoulder. *Nothing*, it thought at her.

Raven frowned and slowly rose from her crouch. The bird faded back to whatever plane it chose to inhabit once her attention on needing it had drifted. It was never far away, even if it wasn't always physically with her. A word would bring it every time.

With a sense of disgust, she cautiously lowered herself back onto her chair, slipped the 9mm away, but kept the icy dagger reversed in her grip. The blade pressed coldly against the underside of her forearm. She preferred blades to firearms anyway.

What kind of pointless test was that?

The door behind her opened and she was out of the chair and over the desk in an instant, her small, wiry fame belying her athleticism and strength. Many had underestimated her physical ability to their detriment.

"It's all right, settle down."

The voice was deep and accented Scottish, but nothing like anything she had known before. Maybe some country accent, or the remnant of an older dialect. Regardless, it wasn't broad enough to give her any trouble understanding, but was instantly recognisable. The man who had recruited her, who she knew only as Boss.

"The fuck is going on?"

He smiled at her, wide and open, teeth bright and large

in his grizzled head. The man was massive, at least six and half feet, wide as a barn door. His iron grey hair was cut almost to the skull, his stubble a sparse snowscape across a square chin. He looked to be about fifty or maybe a little older, but Raven had rarely seen anyone, of any age, as imposing and dangerous. He put her teeth on edge.

"We're testing you."

"The fuck for, you already recruited me."

"Sure, but we don't have to keep you." He held up a hand to stay her burst of outrage, grinning again. "I just wanted to see if you went for hardware or magic first."

"Did I pass?" She felt the twist of her mouth that reminded her of a teenager, not the twenty-five-year-old military professional she was supposed to be. This guy *really* put her on edge.

"You went for a gun, then a maged weapon, then called your familiar. Perfect response sequence, really."

"Being in the army taught me to rely on mundane gear first, and only, if I could. Otherwise too many questions got asked."

"Exactly, and that applies here too, even if I did see your power and invite you in. So, you ready to meet the Squad?"

She shook her head. "You've hardly told me anything about this lot. You don't have to keep me, you said. Do I have to keep you? I want to know more."

"If you don't 'keep us', it's right back to the brig for you."

She shrugged. "Might be a better option." She didn't believe it for a second, but he didn't need to know that.

"Fair enough. I like your attitude. Come on, I'll talk on the way."

Outside the door was another man, clearly waiting for them. He was nearly as big and wide as Boss, his dark skin almost ebony in the low light. His head was shaved bald, glistening, and his smile as wide and welcoming as Boss's had been.

"This is Smoke," Boss said. "He's my right hand man. We started Dark Squad together after I spotted him doing some freaky disappearing act in a rat-infested Middle-Eastern shithole."

"We'd both had enough of orders and military discipline," Smoke said. "And we began to question our directives. I was a Marine, Boss was SAS, we saw a kindred spirit in each other."

Raven walked between the two of them, feeling like a child. She didn't reach either man's shoulder. "But this isn't military, you told me."

"Not officially, no." Boss gestured into a side room off the corridor and she went in. Comfortable sofas and armchairs littered the space, a large screen TV was turned off in one corner. A tall guy with sandy hair and piercing blue eyes sat reading a book. Though nearly the height of Boss and Smoke, he was skinny as a rake handle, but exuded taut strength. He looked to be maybe late-twenties.

"That's Taipan," Boss said.

Taipan looked up, nodded. "G'day. Good to meet ya." His Australian accent was unmistakable.

"You people really say 'G'day'?" Raven asked.

"Not at night so much." He grinned and went back to reading.

Raven thought these people all grinned too damn much.

"And I'm Jet."

Raven turned. Jet was not as short as Raven, but not a giant like the three men. Muscular, solid, with short black hair, olive skin and narrow eyes. She maybe had a decade or so on Raven in age.

"Don't let this cockforest intimidate you."

"I'm not easily intimidated, but I'm glad to see another woman."

"We're all ex-military." Boss pointed around at each of them. "Australian Army, Israeli Special Forces, you already know I was SAS and Smoke was a Marine."

"Hoo fucking rah," Smoke said, and slumped into an armchair.

"Makes my time seem paltry," Raven said.

"No way, you went into the US Army as a teenager, you've got quite a few years of training, and a *hell* of a record. That's what we want." Boss sat and gestured for her to do the same. "You see, after Smoke and I started Dark Squad, we were noticed by a global organisation called Armour. I'm not going into the long boring story now, but the short version is that Armour exists to take care of magical, unnatural, supernatural, etcetera threats to the non-magical, unsuspecting masses. They're like a global magical army, outside any government. Because we have the crack skills with military hardware *and* the mad magical chops greater than most, and because our little Squad started making waves, we got pulled in as Armour's special ops team. We're their black ops, doing all the direct infiltration and wetwork they don't want to see."

"Along with our military and magical skills, we're also all a bit behind on our anger management classes," Smoke said with a wry twist of the mouth. "We work best when we're allowed to kill the bad guys without too much supervision, you get me? But Armour decided we were best off with them instead of maybe, at some point, against them. It's worked well so far."

Raven frowned. "So Armour is a secret organisation and you're a secret within Armour?"

Boss smiled. "Black ops within black ops."

"The blackest ops," Smoke said.

Taipan laughed. "None more black!"

Raven frowned. "Why do I suddenly feel like this outfit's ill-fated fucking drummer?"

Boss shook his head, his face growing serious. "We've long established that five works best, it's an occult number, you know."

Jet waggled her fingers like a sideshow magician. "The points of the pentacle!"

"Stow that shit, Jet. Truth is, you're replacing a dear friend called Blinder, who we lost on the last mission. He'd been with us a long time."

Raven laughed, but there was no humour in it. "No pressure then. Dead man's shoes?"

"You'll be fine. I know how to pick my operatives. We're dealing with the loss of Blinder, but the Squad comes first. And the fact you were prepared to be cut off entirely before you knew the real details of this permanent commission speaks volumes."

"It's not like I'm giving much up," Raven admitted.

"Well, you've gained a lot, trust me," Boss said. "But enough history, we have a pressing mission, which is why you've been called in now. It would have been nice to break you in gently, but there's something to be said for hitting the ground running, yeah?"

"I'm ready."

"Good. This one comes from Commander Giraud in the Paris Armour HQ."

The others in the room switched, their attention total and serious in a moment. Raven smiled softly to herself. They might be a rag tag bunch, but they were tight and focussed. The smile faded as she wondered how long it might take her to fit in. Or if she ever would. Regardless, despite what she'd told Boss, she didn't want to go back to the brig and serve out five years for assault of a fellow soldier. That dick had deserved it, though that was old news and no longer relevant. But she couldn't be locked up, she'd go mad.

"We going to Paris?" Jet asked.

"No, that's just where the orders are from this time," Boss said. "Our target is a necromancer."

And the full weight of her new position fell on Raven like a wet mattress. After a life hiding her magical powers, thinking she was a freak, she found herself surrounded by others with unnatural skills of their own who talked about it openly and without derision.

"Seriously?" Smoke asked.

"Seriously. He's been raising rezzers and placing them in various positions of power, slowly securing all kinds of advantages in business and politics. He's got them in a couple of European governments, several places of power in the Middle East, the CEOs of least three major US corporations that we know of. He's getting way too much influence, playing both sides of wars, collecting huge sums of cash from dozens of conflicting interests. Clever bastard."

Taipan held up a hand. "Wait. What's a fucking rezzer?"

"Resurrected human."

Taipan's eyebrows shot up. "Zombies?"

"No, resurrected humans."

"There's a difference?"

Boss sighed. "They don't teach you much in Alice Springs?"

"You know I'm from fucking Melbourne."

"A zombie is a mindless revenant. It simply wants to eat human flesh, mainly brains, and staggers around with that single purpose, slowly rotting as it goes. And they're not fucking real. A rezzer is a dead fucker raised up with magic. It doesn't breathe or eat or sleep or shit, but it can pretend to do all those things, and it looks and acts like a regular person. Except it is entirely under the thrall of the necromancer who raised it. Regardless of any other influence, the necro's will overrides everything."

"So that's how it infiltrates society," Jet said.

"Exactly. This particular necromancer has either put rezzers into power or found people in power, killed them, and then rezzed them to work for him. They operate exactly like regular people. They conceal the fact of their deadness, and fulfil the necro's orders."

Taipan made a face of grudging respect. "Cunning fucker. But must be powerful as hell to control as many as you suggest."

"Quite. Armour has put out a lot of his fires, taken out a lot of his rezzers, but his power is growing too widespread. Different Armour bases around the world are getting in on it and reporting his feelers reaching their jurisdictions. It's been agreed the necromancer himself has to go down. When he dies, his influence dies with him. His rezzers will all just drop, nothing but empty corpses the moment the necro's life is snuffed out. So Giraud at Armour Paris has taken on the gig and he's deploying us."

"Because this sounds dangerous as hell," Smoke said.

"Exactly." Boss spread a map out on a table and the Squad gathered around to see. "According to Armour intel, our man is holed up in here."

"Is that a castle?" Jet asked. The map showed a hill surrounded by forest. Atop the hill blueprints marked out the rooms and walls of a huge square building with a large open space in the middle.

"Yep, that's Castle ThisGuysFucked. We don't need any more information than that. We're being air-dropped in here." Boss tapped the map, south of the hill.

"Right in the trees?" Smoke said.

"Definitely not Paris," Jet said. "Where is this?"

"Somewhere in the arse end of Belarus, not far from where the border meets with Ukraine and Russia. Deep ancient forests, miles from any civilisation."

"Getting in is one thing, but then how do we get out?"

"Gonna be tricky, but this necro is canny. He'll have transport we can secure, I'm sure, or we might be able to call for an extraction, depending on the lay of the land. No matter, we'll worry about that later. We drop in, we mount the hill, gain the castle and find him. Kill him and somehow get home in time for tea and fucking crumpets. All good?"

"All good," the others said in unison.

Boss looked down at Raven. "All good?"

"I guess so."

He threw his overlarge grin at her. "You're not here to prove yourself, right? You're part of the Squad now, testing is all over, so just accept that and roll with it."

"Okay." Though she felt anything but okay. This was all a hell of a long way from tours of duty in Afghanistan.

They sat in the back of an Armour stealth helicopter, ten minutes out from the drop. Raven felt good back in full fatigues and pack again, weapons strapped across her body. Her knives were close, especially the jade ice dagger, always right there ready. Despite the issues she'd had with command, the trouble hiding her skills, she had loved the fight of active service. Anger management, Smoke had said, and she smiled. Maybe a little more complicated than that, but taking death to shitbags who deserved it was her jam.

"You're a *mudang*?" Jet said suddenly, breaking her reverie.

The question caught her off-guard. "Er, yeah, that's right." How much did the Squad know about her? She knew next to nothing about them and the disadvantage bothered her.

Jet nodded, like she knew exactly what that meant and respected it.

"The fuck is a moo-dang?" Taipan asked.

Raven glanced to the front and Boss and Smoke's broad backs watching over the pilot's shoulder. "We doing this now?"

"Got anything else to do? No offence, just wondering."

Raven forced herself to lighten up. These people were her new family, the enemy was out there. The enemy was always out there, never inside. Remember the mantra. "It's like a Korean shaman, you know. A folk magus. But I grew up in America since I was five, so I hate all that cultural purity bullshit. My magic is rooted in the culture of my birth, but I gathered all kinds of things over the years."

Jet gave a casual thumbs up. "Same for all of us, really. Mixed like colours on an artist's palette, right? Anything of use?"

"Something like that, I guess. What about you?"

"Can it!" Boss strode back into the cabin, Smoke on his heels. "Make ready."

They switched mode in an instant, like Raven had seen before. Wordlessly they went through self-checks then checking each other, lined up, and the door opened. The sound-proofed cabin roared with the rush of air outside, icy cold and buffeting, the rotors chopping the wind into sound bites. They lined up, watched the light flick from red to green, and jumped in quick succession.

It was a low drop and black silk 'chutes opened right away. The thick forest canopy rushed up, far too fast for Raven's liking. She watched between her black boots, adjusted course a little left and right in the hope of coming in between trees and having the best shot at an easy harness escape.

From the sudden roar of the chopper into the cold fall, silence pressed in. She didn't waste any attention on the rest of the Squad, drew hard on the 'chute as her feet crashed into the foliage, pulled her elbows in, tucked her heels against her butt. Crashing and snapping of leaves and branches filled her ears then she bounced and held up, hanging in her harness in utter blackness. She flicked down her night vision goggles and scanned below. The forest floor was about twenty feet down. If it was soft enough she could drop that far and roll.

Leaves and branches burst beside her and Smoke fell into view. His 'chute snagged up a little lower than hers and he looked up, his wide grin pale in the darkness. Then he was gone. The harness hung limp, Smoke had vanished. She caught movement below, looked down and there he was, looking up at her again. Like he'd teleported from one spot to the other. She smiled crookedly. *I guess that's where he gets his name from then.*

"Want me to catch you?" he called up.

"Fuck no!" She hit the harness release, dropped, tucked and rolled through leaf litter and came up into a crouch. It had been a little further than she thought and her heart raced at the prospect of injury, but she was fine.

"Ballsy," Boss said, striding up beside her.

"A little help?"

Jet joined them and the four looked around until they spotted Taipan upside down some thirty feet off the ground, spinning in a gentle figure eight.

Boss sucked air over his teeth. "Fucking hell."

"I got it." Smoke took two or three paces forward then vanished. Several moments later he appeared without breaking stride along a thick limb only a few feet from where Taipan hung. In seconds, with a knife and rope employed judiciously, they were all gathered on the forest floor.

Boss checked his compass and pointed. "That way. No lights, use your night goggles, single file. If anything comes at us, use hand-to-hand if possible. We don't want to warn anyone in that castle we're coming by sending gunfire through the night. Quiet as church fucking mice, all right?"

Without waiting for a response he led the way.

Raven didn't know her natural spot in the Squad, but Boss took point and Jet fell in behind him. Taipan waved her forward, then Smoke took the rear guard, so it seemed she was in the middle. She wondered if Blinder, the dead ex-member, had been in the middle too.

The forest floor was dense with undergrowth and tree roots, reaching up to trap an unwary ankle. The going was slow, machetes deployed left and right. Several times they had to double back and cut a new path when the vegetation became too thick even for chopping. After half an hour, Raven's muscles had a nice burn happening, sweat soaked into her black fatigues. The sixty pound pack wasn't a burden yet, but it would be if they had to keep up this pace and exertion for too long.

A deep moan rose up, drifting through the trees from somewhere ahead. Boss's fist shot up and the Squad froze. Something moaned again, then another off to the left. A third joined it, then a fourth and then there were too many to place and count.

The Squad split their line out wide, scanning left and right through the darkness. Crunching and cracking of leaves and twigs joined the melancholic laments as several somethings shambled towards them.

"Two o'clock," Smoke said, then vanished. He reappeared moments later behind the silhouette of a man and took its head from its shoulders with a single machete stroke.

Then there were figures everywhere, pushing out between the tree trunks, faces slack and groaning, the stench of rotten flesh filled their nostrils.

"They fucking zombies now?" Taipan asked

Jet stepped forward and said, "Sit on the floor."

Her voice was deep, powerful, and the compulsion to drop her ass to the leaf litter was almost too much for Raven to ignore. And the command hadn't even been directed at her.

"Sit down!" Jet ordered again, clearly using more than mere sound, the waves of her voice something beyond the simply auditory. "Not working!" Jet told the Squad, but they could see that for themselves.

Smoke blinked in and out again, machete flashing. Heads rolled.

Taipan crouched, made complicated gestures and barked a short word. Flame shot from his outstretched fingers and engulfed an approaching figure. The attacker went up in flames, flesh and clothes crackling, but didn't slow for a moment.

Taipan pulled a machete free and hacked the burning man down. "Fuggen hell! Flaming zombie attack!"

"Engage and destroy," Boss shouted. "Decapitate for your best chance. Questions later."

Raven chose to ignore the nature of the enemy, treat it like any other, and fell into the dance. Her jade dagger was more than a simple edge, its magic froze everything it cut. Limbs and heads shattered to flesh cubes when they hit hard roots or branches, or she hit them with fists and feet after a stab or slice. The machete in her other hand carved bigger wounds, her ambidextrousness making her into a whirling, scything tiny tornado of death. This is what she lived for, to get in close, to move, dive, duck and weave, cutting anything that strove to interrupt her movement. Nothing was as pure as the slice of a sharp edge.

She caught glimpses of Jet, expert strikes of hands and feet, fighting like some master from a movie, not speaking at all. Smoke popped in and out of sight, appearing randomly to decapitate, then vanish again. Taipan reached and lunged, wiry and fast, chopping two-handed with his machete as though it were a sword. When he took out a leg and the thing fell, he'd lob flame at it to burn it where it lay. Boss slammed all around himself, sometimes lifting the revenants high to smash them down over a bent knee. He left more alive than dead, disabled with destroyed spines and necks, reaching and dragging themselves over the rough ground. The Squad's magic pulsed and flashed, quick-fire spells of speed and protective wards, deployed smoothly with fists and feet and blades. Raven used combat magic of her own, practiced surreptitiously in theatres of war around the world, but realised dimly that she had so much to learn from these people.

In minutes it was over, silence settling but for the gasping of breath as the Squad re-joined one another.

"Anyone hurt?" Boss asked.

"One of the fuckers bit me," Jet said. She held up her left arm, a deep crescent in her wrist leaking thick blood that looked black in the night.

Boss started to dress the wound, rinsing it with saline and disinfectant first. "Anyone else?"

Taipan leaned forward, stared hard at Jet's eyes. "Er, Boss… Were they zombies?"

"There's no such thing, you fucking idiot, I already told you that," Boss said. "She's not going to become one of the walking dead." Something moaned near his foot, a broken man twisted in all the wrong directions, dragging itself one-handed over the ground. Boss slammed a boot into its head, stoved the skull in. The stench of rotten meat swelled in the air.

"You're sure?"

"These are rezzers. They could have been here for years, decades, without the magic refreshed, so they're starting to rot, that's all. There's probably a lot more."

Jet reached up and slapped Taipan's cheek. "Stop being such a buttercup."

Smoke put a hand on Raven's shoulder. "You were quite something to watch there. Like a razor-sharp godsdamned ballerina or something."

The others nodded, smiled agreement.

Raven couldn't help smiling too, wondering if she'd earned her place a little more securely. "It's my gift."

"Fall out," Boss said. "Go wide, and listen for more."

They proceeded more cautiously than before, fanned out across a wider area, eyes peeled. Moaning and guttural coughs erupted now and then, homing in quickly on the Squad. Taipan took out a pair of rezzers with quick double-handed machete strokes.

"I thought you said these things were intelligent like regular people," he said.

Boss stepped sideways, slammed a fist into a rezzers

face, collapsing its head with inhuman strength, then threw a scowl at Taipan. "It's not only the flesh that rots when the magic is left to degrade. The orders remain, but their brains have moulded out too."

Jet grimaced. "That's fucking horrible."

"Yeah. I'm guessing they have two over-riding commands. Stay within a certain area and kill anything that enters that area. The necromancer would check in on his more active thralls, keep the magic fresh and therefore the rezzer would retain its humanity. These ones, he's just left to nature."

Raven shivered at the thought, imagined their active brains understanding their fate as their sense of self slowly decayed. "This is actually a fate worse than death. I thought that was just a figure of speech."

Boss glanced over at her, slight shake of the head. "There are many fates worse than death. Concentrate, people."

Something swung down from a tree limb directly in front of Raven, leering and drooling, it howled as arms thrust forward, fingers wriggling like hard, hungry worms. Raven bit back a yelp of surprise, ducked and slashed upwards. Her jade dagger clipped one arm and it stiffened immediately. She spun to one side, whipped around a heel kick, and the arm shattered into a thousands shards of frozen meat. As the rezzer strained about, its remaining arm clawing at the air, she ducked back under and slammed the dagger into its back. Hard ice spread like a fast-blooming flower across its body and she punched right through, destroying its spine and organs. It fell limp from the tree and she stepped over it.

"Damn fine knife," Smoke said. "You made a rezzer ring donut."

Raven grinned. "Yeah, long story attached to this."

"You'll have to tell me some time."

"Sure."

The night was largely starless and the darkness under the trees wasn't much relieved when they emerged from the densest part of the forest and began the slow climb up the mount on which the castle sat. It loomed over them, massive and foreboding, a black silhouette against the slightly lighter sky. Night goggles on, marked for silence, the Squad crept over rocky ground, hunched low, eyes everywhere.

They gained the foot of the castle wall without incident and Boss gestured to his left. Tight to the huge grey stone blocks, they moved single-file in the wall's shadow towards a corner. As they rounded the corner, they found themselves beside a rectangular lake some twenty feet across that ran along the entire front of the building. Halfway down was a large portico that led to a bridge over the lake that in turn led to an imposing double door.

"A fucking moat," Taipan whispered. "This is like Disney's last nightmare."

"Moat's go all the way around," Smoke said. "This is... a fucking pond, who cares."

"We going in the front door?" Jet asked.

Boss pointed across the bridge. "Those doors are thick and heavy, but it's the only ground level point of entry. Short of some serious grappling or climbing, it's our best bet."

Jet sighed. "We're going in the front door."

Smoke chuckled, low and rumbling. "The time for stealth appears to be over."

"We'll see," Boss said. "This is as little warning as we could give them. We've no idea what we'll find inside. Certainly more rezzers, but who the fuck knows what else. Smoke, you wanna check, let us in?"

"Sure thing."

Smoke vanished.

"The fuck does he keep doing?" Raven asked. "That's some skill."

"He's a planeswalker," Boss said. "He can step from our realm into another and back again. Right now he's walking however far he estimated he needed to go to get to the other side of that door. Then he'll step back into our realm and be inside to open up for us."

"Holy shit."

"Yeah. There's not a cell on earth that can hold Smoke, or a building that can keep him out."

"Where does he go?"

Boss laughed softly. "No idea. He won't say and I've

given up asking."

"Huh. And you throw fire around?" Raven asked Taipan.

"We all have many skills, but my specialty is pyromancy, yeah. And Jet here has a fucking powerful voice of command she can turn on."

"Which is apparently useless against those mindless things." Jet's face was set in frustration.

"A necromancer's commands are designed to always be the foremost thing in any rezzer's thoughts," Boss said. "Seems that even overrides your voice."

"Great."

"And my flames don't even slow them down," Taipan said. "If anything, when they're burning they're more dangerous! Fucking nightmare."

The double doors clunked and one side creaked open. Smoke leaned out with a grin and waved them in. As they hunched to scurry across the bridge Smoke called out, "Don't worry about being careful. There are cameras everywhere in here like mushrooms in a wet field. We've been made."

They stood tall and sprinted to him. As Raven stepped inside she saw the interior was completely at odds with the outside. The ancient fortification housed a modern interior of expensive décor and up-to-the-minute technology. Smoke wasn't lying about the cameras, they sprouted from every wall and corner.

"Get ready to engage," Boss said. "He's sure to send something against us now."

As the words left his mouth, a ravening roar and howl rang through the tall, wide hallways. Then more than one, then dozens and claws skittered and scrabbled on the wooden floors.

"Fucking dogs," Jet said. "I hate it when they make me kill dogs."

"Yeah, not so much dogs," Taipan said.

They turned to see where he was looking. A crowd of huge, leathery creatures with wide maws crammed with sharp teeth tumbled around the corner, clambering over each other in their need to get to the prey first. They bore the barest resemblance to dogs, more like massive dog-shaped beasts with some parody of a crocodile's head. Jaws snapped and slathered. The barking and growling doubled as another crowd of them hurtled around the other end of the hallway.

"Great!" Taipan said. "Dark Squad in a giant teeth sandwich."

"Rain fire!" Boss yelled.

Raven swung her AK47 into play simultaneously with the others and they dropped into a ragged formation. She stood beside Smoke facing one way while Jet, Taipan and Boss faced the other. The corridor exploded into thunder and lightning as the automatic weapons barked and kicked. Armour-piercing ammo filled the air and the leathery flesh of the beasts erupted and split. Raven had a moment to marvel at the accuracy of her team mates. She thought her marksmanship was top notch, but these guys were a class above. Then she was distracted by the realisation that no blood came out of the perfectly placed wounds. The monsters didn't even slow.

"Brains are too fucking small in those giant heads," Boss yelled. "Get the eyes or shoot out the legs!"

But the things were almost on them.

Raven re-sighted, carved full auto low to the ground and took off the legs of the lead two beasts. They went down, still snapping and wriggling as more tumbled over them. The pile-up barely slowed the rest and those behind were already clambering over their fallen. She got a couple of bullseye shots right through eye sockets and two more dropped. Then Smoke blinked out beside her and Raven faced a hoard of monsters on her own.

First mission and this was it. What the fuck even were these things? She'd never imagined anything like them and they were so close she could smell their fetid breath. She let the AK go and pulled the jade dagger. As the one closest lunged for her, she slashed out and leapt up, put one foot to a sturdy table against the wall and flipped. As she turned over in the air she exulted to see the beast she'd slashed falter and collapse. Its head shattered as it hit the ground.

At least the dagger works! she thought, and came down on her knees on the back of another beast.

As it twisted and writhed, teeth slamming together only inches from her leg, she stabbed down into the back of its neck where she hoped some spine might be and leapt again. *I'll show you a fucking ballerina.* She jumped and danced between the beasts, slashing for legs and heads wherever she could. If she stopped moving she was dead, but if she changed direction often enough, and had a little luck, she could avoid the worst of their attack.

As she turned in one leap, she spotted Smoke appear far down the corridor, the other side of Boss, Jet and Taipan and the beasts they were fighting.

"Hey, motherfuckers!" Smoke yelled. Several beasts turned at the sound, then took off after him. Smoke bolted around the corner out of sight.

Boss and Taipan were ducking and shifting, chopping with machetes and firing with high-calibre handguns, taking a decent amount of their enemies down. With the reduced numbers thanks to Smoke's distraction, they gained the advantage and turned to help Raven.

She paid a little more attention to their magic as she kept moving, trying to learn as she cut and froze flesh, moved again. She couldn't count how many there had been or how many she had killed but she suddenly found herself standing alone in the corridor, some distance from where the fight had started. Heaped mounds of dead and broken leathery flesh lay between her and Boss and the others. Beyond them, more fallen beasts. Several of the things still snapped weakly and writhed, bodies quivered, but none had the ability to attack any more, spines severed or brains crushed.

"Rezzed fucking hellhounds," Boss said. "As if the fuckers aren't bad enough alive. Who's hurt?"

"Who isn't?" Jet asked.

Raven felt warmth over her left hand and looked down. Blood ran in rivulets from her sleeve. Her arm just below the elbow was opened in a wide gash. As she noticed it, the pain set in. She knew that once the adrenaline eased it would only get worse. She looked up, lifted the arm. "Err..." Then everything went black.

Raven came around to Boss's voice. "...be all right. You know he can take care of himself."

"Sure, but let's hope he can find us again." That was Jet.

Raven opened her eyes. Boss had dressed her arm, the others had a variety of bandages on arms, legs, heads. Taipan had half his head covered, his left eye obscured by dressings. But they all seemed in good enough spirits.

"Welcome back."

Raven looked at Boss, felt her cheeks redden. "Fucking hell, I can't believe I passed out."

"They have venom and you're not inoculated," Boss said. "Well, you are now. You'll feel queasy for a while, and you lost some blood, but you'll be okay."

A spent syringe lay on the ground beside her. Boss glanced at it. "Yeah. One of many parts of our standard medkit. They're a bit different to what you're used to."

"No shit."

She sat up, and did indeed feel quite nauseated. She took a few slow, deep breaths, felt herself slowly centring again.

"Now I need your help," Boss said. "You operational?"

No way would Raven say anything but yes to that question on her first mission. "What do you need?"

"Your little friend. We need a recon mission, find out where the target is. We spend too long fucking around here with his pets and we're giving him time to slip away."

"You got it."

Raven spoke the word and the *samjok-o* stepped onto her shoulder. "We know what this guy looks like?"

Boss pulled a grainy photo from his pocket. It wasn't much, clearly taken at full zoom, it showed a Caucasian man, perhaps somewhere in his forties, cropped dark hair and a linen suit. "That enough?"

Raven took the photo. "It'll have to be." She stared at it, made sure the three-legged raven familiar took a good look too, then asked it to go fetch for her.

The *samjok-o* took wing and vanished. Raven closed her eyes and stayed with its thoughts. It did nothing for her nausea, flitting in and out of existence, room to room, searching the vast, sprawling complex. Then it found him, stood in the middle of a huge protective circle in the open courtyard at the centre of the castle.

She thanked her friend and opened her eyes. "Looks like he's waiting for us," she said.

As they moved out, Boss radioed Smoke but got no response. When Jet cast a hooded look at him he just shook his head and jogged on. Raven worried how they might feel if something bad had befallen Smoke. They had only recently lost Blinder and that clearly bore down on them heavily. To lose another so soon would be more than harsh. Then again, if Smoke were dead and needed to be replaced, at least she wouldn't be the new kid any more. It was a mercenary thought, but mildly comforting, especially as she hardly knew Smoke. But she had already grown to like the man a lot. She wanted to tell him the story of her dagger.

Come on, you fucker, she thought to herself. *Let's all go home from this one.*

They tracked their way through an ostentatious ballroom, eyes sweeping left and right, alert for further attack. But everything seemed still. Almost too still, if Raven believed in clichés. It was as though the castle itself was waiting for something. For some trigger to be tripped.

"I'm on fucking edge here," Taipan said. "I don't like having no depth perception."

"Your eye going to be okay?" Raven asked.

He shrugged. "It's still there. Whether it'll be okay or not remains to be seen." He grinned and looked down at her. "Remains to be fucking seen! Geddit?"

She couldn't help a laugh escaping, shook her head. "You people are..." She couldn't find the word.

"All right?" Boss threw back over his shoulder. "Is that what you meant?"

And she realised it was. "Yeah. You people are all right."

Boss nodded without looking around. "Wind it up, now.

Let's concentrate."

The ballroom led into an ornate dining room. Polished rosewood table, intricate chandeliers and expensive-looking artworks. The table was laid with enough silver to pay off the national debt of some island nations.

"Looks like the fucker is planning a party." Boss pointed to a door on the far side. "That way."

The door had glass panels, light net curtains inside and wan moonlight beyond. They vaguely made out bushes and a stone fountain.

"Seems the cloud cover has cleared a bit," Jet said.

They slowed, took their weapons up in a casual ready position and advanced slowly. As they neared the doors, there was a click and they swung open. Boss paused, then straightened up. "Seems we're expected."

He strode out into the courtyard.

The others gathered beside him. The courtyard was huge, maybe a hundred metres across. It had garden beds and shrubbery all round, mostly Italian in style. Stone fountains sprayed and burbled all over, everything lit in monochrome by the half moon now clear of clouds. What had once no doubt been a central pond was now a raised dais of stone. The circular edge was old granite, carved with runes and sigils of protection. It crackled with power, warding pretty much everything a mage could throw at it. Raven had never felt such concentrated magic in her life. The man in the linen suit stood in the centre, arms casually at his sides.

"Hello, there," he said, his voice heavily accented Eastern European. "I have to admit, I'm impressed you got this far."

Boss raised his AK and squeezed the trigger. Nothing happened. He frowned, looked at the weapon, then back at the necromancer. "I expected your wards to stop the bullets, not render this entirely inoperative."

"More fool you."

"I guess so."

The air crackled with tension and magic. Raven found herself useless, impotent. Their firearms were inert, the target was caged against their magic. It was a sudden and seemingly insurmountable stand-off.

"Let's hope you're better at hand-to-hand than you are at recognising wards," the necromancer said.

Movement from either side sent a ripple of alertness through them. The square between the necromancer and the Squad filled with black-clad, fast-moving figures. Some flipped and tumbled as they ran in an ostentatious display of athleticism.

Boss groaned.

Taipan made a tight sound in his throat. "Are you fucking serious? Undead fucking ninjas now? They're rezzers, right?"

"Almost certainly," Boss said, his voice tired.

The rezzers gathered in a group, at least twenty of them. Raven looked around, realising that beside the bushes and fountains there was little to no cover. This fucker seemed to have an endless supply of minions.

"Remember," Boss said. "Take out the spine, brain, or decapitate. No amount of incidental damage will slow them. And it looks like they'll be a far greater challenge than the abominations in the forest."

As the Squad crouched, ready for the enemy to rush forward, a door on the far side of the courtyard slammed back.

"Hey, motherfuckers!" Smoke, grinning like the Cheshire cat, lobbed something in a high arc.

"Fire in the hole!" Boss yelled and the Squad hit the deck.

Smoke's grenade sailed high and dropped into the midst of the massed ninjas even as their voices shouted warnings to each other. They began to scatter, some leaping away in time, but the concussion of the blast whined everything to silence for a moment as bright light flashed out. Body parts rained down among chunks of earth and stone.

"That should even the odds a bit," Smoke called.

The massed group of rezzed ninjas had been spread wide by the blast. They yelled at each other over the following silence, trying to regroup. Even the necromancer looked concerned.

"Engage!" Boss hollered, and Dark Squad sprang into

action.

They sprinted in different directions, ensuring the rezzers couldn't regroup. Raven headed for a clutch of three, jade dagger in hand. These were definitely not the mindless, broken things from the forest. The way they moved, communicated, readied themselves, showed them to be every bit as alert and dangerous as an enemy could get, only far harder to hurt. At least the dagger gave her a distinct advantage.

She heard Smoke's high-pitched laughter as she engaged the first assailant, then nothing existed but her own fight. The ninjas were fast, faster than any enemy she'd met before. The first kick came at her so suddenly it clipped her ribs before she could dodge fully, forced most of her air out. The shock of being hit so easily winded her more than the impact, but she managed to swipe the dagger across and felt it drag through flesh. The ninja put his foot down and his leg crumbled, sent him tumbling to the ground. She was already past him, blocking a furious flurry of blows from the next, barely twisted as the third threw another kick. The one she had cut was up on one leg already, hopping expertly to re-engage. She was hurt and still all three faced her.

Raven took a deep breath and whispered the word to her *samjok-o*. She asked for help and the three-legged bird stepped into the air again followed by a cloud of other shining black avians. They swirled and mobbed the ninjas, interrupting their approach. Raven let her mind slip into the state of *wu wei*, a Taoist concept of non-being. Her mind removed itself from her actions and she let pure training and instinct take over. No longer trying to learn or emulate, she let her magic flow as she danced with the flock of ravens, knives in hand, a lyrical, swirling display of athletic grace and deadly accuracy. As the birds dipped, she rose, as they fanned out, she dove in. The rezzed ninjas scored hits here and there, but she put off that pain for later. She felt the occasional searing burn of a blade strike and ignored that too. Her own dagger swept and flew, shattered flesh raining around in musical accompaniment to the dance.

Once her three assailants were gone, she moved with

her cloud of birds across the courtyard, engaging wherever there was movement not of her Squad. Howls and shouts, cries and slaps of flesh on flesh, and then stillness.

Arms out to either side, the dagger held low in one hand, hair come loose and hanging over her eyes, Raven stopped moving. Statue-still but for the fast rise and fall of her chest, the rasp of rapid breathing. She let the emptiness drain away from her, slowly raised her eyes to look around.

Boss and Taipan stood side by side, hurt but smiling. Smoke strolled across the courtyard towards them. Raven's eyes fell on Jet, sat back against a fountain, bleeding and bruised, one eye already swollen shut. Jet gave a shaky thumbs up as she hauled herself to her feet.

The Squad regathered and stood before the protective circle. In its centre, the necromancer looked shaken.

"What's next?" Boss asked.

"You people are tenacious," the necromancer said. "But let's see you face this." He began chanting, knotted his fingers into complicated signs and mudras.

"He's summoning something," Jet said, slightly slurred through swollen lips.

Smoke tilted his head to listen. "A demon, I think," he said with a smile.

Raven's eyes widened. A demon? Seriously? And why were they all so casually amused about that.

"Oh ho," Boss said. "This'll be fun."

As the necromancer's words gained strength, rapidly blurring together, Boss raised his arms as if in supplication. With a rush of burning hot air, he faded and vanished. Before Raven had drawn a shocked breath, Boss reappeared inside the protective circle, standing right before the necromancer.

The necromancer's eyes went wide, his mouth fell open. "What the hell?"

"You really should consider," Boss said. "If you plan to summon a demon, it's best to know who's already around, otherwise what you expect to appear outside might already be there, and then your spell simply reverses itself."

Boss whipped his hand around, grip tight on the hilt of his machete, and the necromancer's head sailed up off his shoulders, spinning over and over, still wearing its expression of shock and disbelief. The body crumpled to the floor at Boss's feet.

Boss looked down at the body for some time as the magic of the protective circle drained away, then he turned and strolled back to the Squad. "There we go then."

"You're a fucking demon?" Raven asked. Her heart beat faster at this revelation than all the fighting up until this point.

Boss shook his head, slipped his machete away. "It's really not as simple as all that. Perhaps I'll try to explain it to you one day. Bad luck for him though, eh?"

Raven looked around the group. They all smiled and she felt like they were all in on a joke to which she wasn't privy. It was frustrating, but she supposed there was an awful lot to learn about these people.

Boss turned to look at the raised dais with its ring of carved sigils. "That's big enough for a chopper to put down, don't you think?"

"I would say so," Smoke agreed.

Boss turned to Jet. "Call it in, please. Tea and crumpet time."

They were taken to an Armour base in Berlin to have their wounds taken care of. Taipan needed to wear a patch for a few weeks but was told he had been lucky and would retain his sight. Other than several dozen stitches between them and a few set bones, they weren't in too bad shape. Some of the Armour mages used a few less than natural techniques to hurry their healing along.

By the time they were in a comfortable lounge being fed, it seemed to Raven that the whole encounter had been weeks ago instead of hours.

"It'll be good to get back to New York," Taipan said.

"There's a young man I know there who'll be very impressed with my eye patch. I've got this whole story about defending myself from a mugging to earn his sympathy."

"Don't you ever think about anything but sex?" Jet asked.

"I think about fighting a lot."

She laughed. "Fair point."

Boss crammed in the last of a sandwich and stood. "Right, I'm going to Paris to debrief with Commander Giraud. You lot head home, I'll see you in Manhattan. Except you, Raven. You're with me."

She frowned. "Everything okay?"

"Yeah. I want him to know how well you did, and for you to see a bit more of Armour operations."

It wasn't too long a chopper ride to Paris and the Armour HQ there. They went through a command centre with computer banks, busy personnel, a large round desk in the middle with holographic projections hovering over it.

"It's like the bridge of the fucking Enterprise," Raven said.

Boss laughed. "Armour has been around since the Crusades, fighting evil and gaining wealth and power. Come on."

He went along a hallway to a door marked *Commander* and knocked.

"Come."

Inside was a large office, filing cabinets and a sofa on one side. Behind a large mahogany desk sat a short man with dark, intense eyes and jet black hair. His face was deeply wrinkled, showing age that seemed to go beyond any mortal lifespan. Raven had no idea why, but she sensed immense power about him. It would take some experience and skill to be an Armour Commander after all, she supposed.

"Aha, Boss, please sit," Giraud said. His French accent was strong, but something else was in there too. Something Slavic maybe. "It all went well?"

"It wasn't easy," Boss said. "But you know us. We prevail."

"You hit some tough resistance?"

Boss nodded slowly. "We really did. The enemy were

immune to Jet's voice, fire barely slowed them down, it's almost like they were the perfect thing to throw at us. Especially without Blinder and his skills. But like I said, we prevail."

Giraud smiled. "Indeed you do. You are a very reliable squad."

"Almost too reliable?" Boss asked.

The air in the room electrified, a sudden tension that put Raven on edge. She had no idea what had just happened, but the friendly greeting seemed distant as a new, icy atmosphere rippled up.

"Too reliable?" Giraud asked.

"You really didn't expect us to make it back, did you?" Boss said. "I mean, those were some pretty massive odds." He gestured at Raven. "Without our new recruit here, we would have had some serious trouble."

Giraud nodded, flicked a quick smile at Raven. "I must admit, I didn't know you had replaced Blinder already."

"Yeah, I thought not. I find it helps to play my cards close to my chest, even with the people supposedly on my side."

"Supposedly?"

Raven saw Giraud's hand move surreptitiously and press at something under his desk. Her own hand drifted close to the jade dagger.

"Why didn't that necromancer bleed when I took his fucking head off, eh?" Boss asked.

Giraud's eyebrows rose. "Didn't bleed?"

"You think I wouldn't fucking notice a small detail like that? That the necromancer supposedly behind all this was a fucking rezzer?" Boss's voice rose in volume with each word.

The door behind them opened and two large Armour operatives stepped in. Giraud began to rise from his chair and Boss's hand came up with a Magnum .44 and blew the Commander's head into mincemeat. It burst like a melon, spraying the wall behind the desk with blood and bone and brains.

Shocked shouts and movement erupted outside the office. As Giraud's body collapsed back into his chair one of the operatives who had come in fell to the ground like a puppet with its strings cut. The other, reaching for Boss, paused, staring open-mouthed.

Boss raised both hands and let the Magnum clatter onto Giraud's desk. "He was the real necromancer," he said loudly as people crowded into the room. "The fact that one of his rezzers dropped when he did is proof of it. Now I realise there's a lot of paperwork to do, but let's all just calm down, yeah? No one else needs to get hurt."

Tension drained slightly, giving way to shock. Hurried conversations travelled out across the base like a wave.

"Better get the Deputy Commander in here," Boss said.

The operative who had come in with the rezzer nodded. "I'll go and make the call."

Raven looked from the Commander's corpse to the dropped rezzer operative, mind reeling as she figured out the course of events. Her eyes finally reached Boss to find him smiling at her.

"You see why I brought you along now, then? Give you a better idea of our role in all this. You can see why we're needed?"

She smiled. "Black ops within black ops?"

Boss laughed. "None more black."

THE
THROAT

Originally published in SNAFU: Last Stand.

The Throat

Jack Warren had every intention of running for his life, but his foot shot sideways in the pool of viscera that only moments before had been digesting Tom Johnson's last meal. The rest of Johnson had been carried away. Instead of turning tail, Warren faceplanted in the warm, recently spilled entrails of his friend. He sat up, brought his assault rifle to bear, inadvertently lifting a loop of Johnson's intestine over the barrel. Through the gore pouring down his face, deafened by automatic fire exploding all around him, Warren had a moment to see the giant creature bear down. The size of a small car, fat and rounded, thick muscles rippled under taut, maroon skin. A huge, blood-red maggot, it powered along the jungle floor at uncanny speed, rapid peristaltic movement undulating its flesh. Its seemingly blind face split open, half a dozen interlocking tusks separating outwards and tipping forward to reveal a wide circular mouth forested with row after row of diamond sharp teeth disappearing down a deep, wet gullet.

Warren got off a short blast of fire, then the thing's lower right tusk, as long as his forearm, punched into his face between the eyes.

The beast didn't slow.

The sharp bone burst from the back of Warren's head as it slithered on as fast as a fit man might jog. Warren was lifted and swept along, his corpse dragging at the fat worm's side like a rag as it plunged through thick foliage. The creature shook its front end like a wet dog shaking its head, then bent up in the center even as it moved on, and Warren was flipped up and into the wide round maw. He vanished, a momentary extra bulge in the thing's rapidly pulsing body.

"Fall the fuck back!" Jimenez yelled over the roar of .45 caliber automatic fire, aware of fear evident in his deep, strong voice. The squad backed up as one, between the trees dotted across the valley floor, firing as they went.

Behind the dark red maggot that had swallowed

Warren, hundreds more surged up , over the bullet-lacerated bodies of their brethren. They moved like an undulating sea, rushing forward at frightening speed, sometimes rolling, no particular concern about which part of them was up. Hundreds of rounds ripped through the air to meet them, tracers flashing through the gloom under the canopy, bursting ichorous green splashes from the fat sides of the creatures. The first few shots seemed to barely slow the things, but enough firepower eventually split them open to burst and leak and writhe on the leafy ground. But still more came.

"Spread out!" Jimenez called, and the squad fanned wide, crossfire ripping the giant maggots to shreds. The gulping worms consumed their own kind in massive swallows even as they slid over them, growing with everything they ate. "This is for Warren and Thomson!" Jimenez screamed, his rage incandescent, and every assault rifle echoed his sentiment.

Crimson flesh and thick green blood slicked the jungle floor, but still the wave of maggots rolled on, an all-consuming tide.

"Where's the end of it?" Gemmell yelled.

Jimenez's squad of eight was already down to six and he had no intention of losing any more.

"Grenades!" he barked, and the rack and pump of mounted grenade launchers sent explosives flying. Designed to pierce armor more than 300mm thick, the sudden wall of explosions had the desired effect and tore the flood of maggots to shreds. Among the smoke and sizzling meat, a strange quiet fell.

"The fuck was that?" Ichiro asked in his low, quiet way.

"Warren and Thomson, gone," Shackleton said, her voice almost as low as Ichiro's.

"I told my little girl this was a routine investigation," Jimenez said firmly into the momentary lull. "I told her I would be back for her birthday on Saturday. I have every intention of riding a fucking pony with my little girl this weekend. Does anyone have any objection to that?"

"Maybe the fucking pony," Salisbury said, her face split

in a grin.

Jimenez barked a laugh. Given he was six foot seven and close to three hundred pounds, she had a point.

Their laughter was a mask, a shield against the sudden and horrible deaths of their friends, and Jimenez knew they needed it. He opened his mouth to call them to order but was interrupted by Ichiro.

"More coming," he said, field glasses at his eyes. "A lot. And by a lot, I mean a fuck ton."

"What the hell are they, Cap?" Haversham asked, his posh English accent incongruous as always among the rest of the squad.

"The fuck I know? They never told me anything about this."

"What did they tell you?"

Jimenez scoffed. "Not a whole lot, it turns out. We need to find where they're coming from. This time we'll be ready. Stay wide, we move forward and meet them."

"Fast, giant, carnivorous maggots?" Shackleton asked, her eyebrows riding high under a short, dark brown bob that poked out from the edges of her helmet. "Seriously, Cap?"

Gemmell, the only squad member bigger than Jimenez, looked from her to his Cap with eyebrows raised. If Gemmell was spooked...

Jimenez raised his hands. "You want boring, go work for the DMV. You want excitement, stick with me. We lost Warren and Thomson to a surprise attack. Let's not lose any more. Stay sharp."

12 HOURS AGO

What kind of experiments?" Jimenez asked.

The bald man behind the desk, gut straining the buttons of his suit, made a rueful face. "I'm afraid I can't tell you too much."

"But it ain't legit, or the Army would go in, the government. You guys are covering your asses, that's why we get the call. So, Mr Cantrell, if you want me to put my team in harm's way, I need intel."

Cantrell pursed his lips for a moment. Jimenez folded his massive arms across his chest and sat back, immovable. Cantrell sighed. "Very well. Honestly, I don't know much about the finer details, not my department, but our organization has been financing some cutting-edge scientific research."

"Deep in the Amazon jungle?"

"The sort of research we'd rather no one else knew about. Let me put it this way: the facility in question is called the DDS, which stands for the Department of Dimensional Sciences. They explore interdimensional interstices and universal nexus points, so I'm sure you can imagine the interest that might garner from certain… authorities."

Jimenez raised his eyebrows. "They explore what the fuck now?"

Cantrell carried on as if Jimenez hadn't spoken. "We've lost contact with our facility down there. I imagine it's been overrun by rebels, something like that. The jungle is a lawless place. Something simple, but nonetheless dangerous. We need your team to go in, clean up, and secure the facility. That's all."

"Clean up and secure, huh?"

"That's all."

"You got any more details of the possible threat?"

Cantrell shook his head. "The facility is situated in a narrow valley. It's steep-sided, a waterfall at one end, so it's a gorge, a deep, rocky dead end. You can only access the valley from a pass between high cliffs at the northern end, but otherwise it's sheer rock faces all around, narrow at the pass, wide at the other end where our facility is built. Good for security, for privacy, but obviously bad for visual access. Our satellite imagery can't see in there."

"What else aren't you telling me?"

Cantrell smiled. "Astute."

"Yep, and I have cute ass too. What are you holding back?"

"There's magnetic interference of some kind. It's been steadily building since we lost contact, further hampering our attempts to see or hear from them. We assume some equipment has gone on the fritz. So we called you."

"To clean up and secure."

"Precisely. You'll be in and out in no time."

Jimenez nodded. "That right?" Cantrell wasn't so good at hiding his lying ass behind that condescending smile. If this went bad, Jimenez would come back and cut those smiling lips off the asshole's face, maybe eat them with eggs for breakfast. "It's my little girl's eighth birthday on Saturday, and I ain't missing that."

"Captain Jimenez, it's only Wednesday. You'll be fine."

NOW

"Here they come!" Ichiro had already moved to one side and hunkered down with ammo packs to either side.

They'd made it another half a mile down the valley. The others picked their spots in time to see the front of the next assault appear between the trees. Weapons fire thundered again as they began decimating the oncoming wave.

"Interesting observation," Ichiro shouted over comms. "They can't climb. The valley slopes up either side, getting steeper until it meets the cliff walls. Every time they try to go up the valley sides, they reach a certain incline then just roll back down. It doesn't slow them, but it keeps them on the valley floor."

Jimenez nodded. "Okay, that's the first good news we've had since my wife woke me early this morning with crude intentions."

A grenade from Shackleton blew a wide gap in the

advance, then she said, "Well, that was only good news for you, Cap."

"Yeah, not us or even your poor wife get any joy from that," Gemmell said, dropping to one knee to change out mags.

"Not true, witches and warlocks," Jimenez gritted his teeth and managed to gun down three maggots in a row. More slowed briefly behind to swallow their dead. "When I'm satiated, I become a much kinder Captain to your sorry asses. You should all send my wife a thank you note and some chocolates."

"I'll send her one of those *With Deepest Sympathies* cards people use for funerals," Haversham said in his posh accent, then his words turned to a furious roar as he went full auto for several seconds.

Jimenez sucked in a breath. "Focus, people! We can't let any of these fuckers get by us. If they get out into the wider jungle, they'll run rampant and cause a whole lot of damage. We came here to find out why the base lost contact, but we find ourselves in a containment situation. If they get past us that's a whole lot of fucked up-ness, agreed?"

"Yes, Sir," they chorused.

The squad moved in a synchronized dance, covering each other, crossfire holding the wave back. Crimson meat fell and blood surged up, and still more came.

"Die, fucking maggots!" Salisbury screamed, her voice high.

Rounds streaked through the hot air tearing chunks from the worms. Their long, bony tusks snapped and spun away, thick green blood sprayed and splattered as red flesh was torn apart, but the maggots were unperturbed. They might momentarily slow as one of them fell, but the wave bunched and then surged over the top. Grenades flew, pumped and thrown up and over the front ranks. Chunks of deep scarlet flesh tumbling in geysers of green viscera, burst into the air along with rocks and earth and thick, waxy foliage. As the bodies piled up, the worms stretched their maws wide and swallowed up the crimson barricade of their dead, barely slowed by the process. Their bodies pulsed and flexed, contracted and extended, growing as they swept up the shallow incline.

As Jimenez quickly switched in a fresh mag, he looked up through the trees. In the distance he saw swirling dark clouds of indigo and purple, forks of bright lightning arcing and crackling inside. *What the fuck is all this?* he had a moment to think, then turned his attention back to carving up the inexorable worm tide.

1 HOUR AGO

"We're getting interference in readings." Barnes's voice was tinny in Jimenez's earpiece.

Jimenez made his way to the cockpit, past the team strapped into webbing on either side of the heavily customized Boeing C-17 Globemaster III. His plane was his pride and joy, deftly liberated from a drug lord in Nicaragua with a personal fortune more than the GDP of some countries. Not that it was any good to the guy now, given he was in several pieces and long eaten by bugs, no doubt.

As Jimenez passed, he glanced at the webbed stacks of cargo locked into place between them: twelve cases of old Spanish CETME Model L assault rifles, six cases of M67 frag grenades, two-thousand pounds of C4 in stacked M112 demolition bricks, eight long cases, each holding a 50-caliber M2 Browning, about three tons of various caliber munitions for everything from semi-automatic handguns to 50-cal, a few cases of mortars and surface-to-air rockets, and, at the back, an armored jeep. He really needed to figure out what to do with this bonus stash from the recent Honduras thing. It was all worth a small fortune if he could only find the right market for it. "What kind of interference?" he asked Barnes, leaning on the back of the pilot's seat.

"Not sure, but instruments are glitching. Probably the

magnetics you were warned about." Barnes looked back over his shoulder, gave a shrug. His face was still tanned from the recent leave he'd enjoyed, three weeks on a Caribbean island with the young woman he'd just married.

Jimenez thought he wouldn't mind a few weeks on a white sand beach himself right about now. "How close are we?" he asked.

"Almost there, but I'm reluctant to push too far if we don't have to."

Jimenez nodded. "You want us to drop early?"

"If possible, Cap. You're about a half hour's hike from the target right now, maybe less."

"Good enough. Loop here, we'll drop, then you head back Manaus. I'll radio in if we need you back. You might need to bring a chopper to lift us out."

Barnes nodded. "Good luck, Cap. And happy camping."

Less than two minutes later the team were parachuting down towards the dark green canopy, two pallets of supplies ahead of them.

On the ground, Jimenez said, "Remember the philosophy, witches and warlocks?"

"Expect no trouble," the squad said in unison, "but bring all the ammo you can carry!"

"You got it! The camping gear and food can stay here until we get back. Arm up and move out."

"Back in time for supper?" Gemmell asked.

"You got it," Jimenez said. "Barnes can cook us up one of his world-famous hot chilis for dinner. Then Haversham'll read you a bedtime story. His lovely voice'll put you right out"

"How about Winnie The Pooh?" Haversham asked, and the way he pronounced Pooh made them all laugh. "Heathens!" he muttered, though he grinned along.

They set out south, expecting no trouble, but armed for a war.

NOW

Jimenez's ears rang from the thunder of gunfire and grenades. The stink of burning meat and the acrid stench of their blood drifted on the breeze blowing up the valley. But they'd stopped the carnivorous tide again. The squad stood panting, checking gear. They were already dangerously low on ammo, but how many more of these things could there be?

Over the tops of the trees, at the distant end of the valley, the mass of dark, bulging clouds he'd seen earlier had grown. More lightning crackled and burst through it. The wind pushing the stench up the valley increased, driven ahead of that unnatural storm.

"Will there be any more?" Salisbury's voice held a tinge of panic Jimenez had never heard before as she echoed his concerns. She was a badass, usually unshakable.

"Don't know."

"Also," Ichiro said, "do you think these *are* a kind of maggot? Or a kind of worm?"

Jimenez frowned. "Both and neither maybe. Does it matter?"

"Maybe. A worm is a worm, but a maggot is the second stage of something else. Something bigger. Egg, then larva, then what?"

"Well, fuck me, thanks for your cheery observations, Ichiro. Let's just murder the fuck out of any we see and then we don't need to know, right? Come on, let's move."

As they jogged on, Jimenez turned his attention to the most immediate problem.

We don't have anything like enough ammo for another fight like that.

Salisbury's tone of panic was borne of the same knowledge, and the rest of the squad would have realized it too. He switched his radio channel over, hoping for the best.

"Barnes, you copy?"

"Go ahead, Cap," the pilot said. "You finished already?"

"Not even close. You still airborne."

"Yep."

"How long to get back here?"

"Get back, Cap?"

"I need an ammo drop toot sweet."

"Holy shit. And there was me planning to masturbate and nap when I got back. Okay, I'm turning now. I'd say about an hour to get back to you?"

Jimenez shook his head. "Can you engage the warp engines and make it quicker? And fuck the interference, I need you right here. I want the ammo dropped on top of us."

Barnes's voice gained the clipped edge of determination. "Shit, okay. I'll do all I can, Cap. On my way."

As they moved further up the valley, the winds from the storm became buffeting and the air beneath the clouds looked dark and electric.

"Let's get up the valley side," Jimenez said. "I want to see this place before we get any closer. We need to know what's down there. And how many more maggots might be milling around." Surely what they'd already fought had to be the last of them. How many could there be in a finite space?

They explore interdimensional interstices and universal nexus points... He shook the thought from his head and ran on.

As they made their way up the steepening incline of the valley side, they spread out into pairs. Jimenez and Gemmell on point, Ichiro and Shackleton behind, with Salisbury and Haversham bringing up the rear. Once they got a few hundred yards up, able to see over the trees to the end of the deep scar in the landscape, they stood in stunned silence for several seconds.

"Jesus fucking Christ," Haversham said eventually.

Jimenez tore his eyes from the spectacle in front of them to glance at the Englishman's pale face. Haversham was no prude, but Jimenez had never heard the man swear before, which was more than unusual given their company. But if there was ever a time to start cursing, this was it. "What the fuck is that?" he asked, returning his gaze to the sight before them.

They stood on a steep, rocky scree some five hundred yards above the valley floor, cliffs at their backs. Ahead, the highest part of the dead-end tear in the earth towered above them, a waterfall tumbling down. In the depths of the valley's end, it seemed physics no longer existed. Evidence of the secret facility was visible, the last few buildings broken and burning around a massive hole in the ground. But 'hole' was nowhere near description enough.

A massive circular rift, wet and glistening, plunged down into the earth. A seemingly living thing, a giant pulsating gullet some hundred yards across. The top of it slowly but continuously prolapsed up and out, folding over itself as it rose. As it curled into the valley, it immediately dried and crumbled, forming a kind of caldera of its own meat. The sides of the quivering gullet were covered with wide rings of rounded pustules, one ring every few hundred feet going down the energetic vessel. As the throat bulged up and crumbled down, another ring of pustules reached the crater's edge and they all burst, hundreds more maggots born, twisting and writhing as if burning on a hot plate before they sensed their purpose and surged up the valley.

The waves Jimenez and the squad had just fought were one thing, and even should there be another, the odds were maybe not insurmountable, especially with an ammo drop. The squad could finish that many. And now that next wave had indeed been born, hundreds more carnivorous crimson worms writhing into existence over the edges of the vomiting throat.

But down its glistening depths were ring after ring after ring of swollen pustules, mile after mile, as far as they could see. Already hundreds more maggots were in the valley, sliding and surging up towards the pass that would release them into the wider world, and there were millions more in the throat, a galactic maw endlessly puking out destruction. In the farthest depths of it a swirling void emanated a bone-chilling cold and absolute blackness, leading to who knew where or what.

Jimenez rocked with vertigo at the sight of it, as though its very presence could pluck him from the valley side and send him falling into eternity forever. Above it all, the unnatural storm raged and roiled, dark blue and purple clouds rippling with white lighting, the static making their hairs stand on end. Jimenez recalled Ichiro's question: *Egg, then larva, then what?* Apart from the devastation they might cause in the wider world in this form, what might they become next if they got out?

"There's no way we can contain this," Shackleton said, her voice shaking in shock and terror. "No one could contain it. It's only a matter of time before they overrun everything."

"Is it getting wider?" Gemmell asked.

"Yes," Ichiro said. "Very slowly, but it's widening with every wave, I think. How big might it get?"

"There's not really anything to stop it growing," Haversham said. "I mean, look at the thing! What rules could ever govern that?"

"Get back down!" Jimenez barked. "We have to get in front of that next lot of maggots before they reach the pass. We have to hold this place, stop any of those fuckers getting out of the valley."

"Cap," Haversham started, "this is–"

"Now!"

"Yes, Sir!" As one, the squad turned back and began to run.

"Ichiro," Jimenez said, "we still have those mines?"

"Yes, Cap."

"Okay, you and Shackleton get directly down and lay mines. We need to disrupt the front of the next wave as much as possible. Then fall back to us. With any luck, we'll have an ammo drop by the time you get there."

Ichiro and Shackleton peeled off to the left while the rest ran on, talking quickly as they ran.

Jimenez switched channels again. "Barnes, we need you now!"

"I didn't stop for a wank. I'm just a few minutes from the valley, coming in low. Ammo crates ready to drop. Where do you need 'em?"

Jimenez looked down into the valley and saw Ichiro and Shackleton start laying mines. The wave of maggots was barely a hundred yards behind them.

"They're too close!" Gemmell yelled, even as Jimenez came to the same conclusion.

His gut clenched. "They're buying us time," he said. "Mad, beautiful bastards. *Run!*"

The squad pounded on, trying to get as far ahead of the wave as possible.

"Barnes, you're gonna see the valley light up in a second. Drop the ammo five hundred yards before that."

"Yes, Sir. What the fuck is that storm I see ahead?"

"The target, Pilot. Drop the ammo, then turn tail and radio in an airstrike. I don't care how you convince whoever you need to convince, but break into government channels and get us a strike. We need big fucking ordinance right under that storm. The end of this valley needs to disappear in fire and rock. We'll hold it in until then."

"Will we?" Gemmell asked.

Jimenez threw him a desperate look. "We have any choice?"

Gemmell didn't get to answer because the mines went up, explosions of noise and dirt and red flesh filled the air.

As the squad hit the valley floor, they heard the distant roar of the C-16's engines. Moments later the big plane powered over them. Jimenez spotted the white domes of the ammo crate parachutes dropping between the trees a couple of hundred yards further ahead. They tried to run faster.

"I hope that drop was in the right place," Barnes said over the comm. "My instruments are fritzed and I'm doing everything by eye and feel."

"It's bang on target," Jimenez said. "I'm sure your new wife is very happy with your ability to hit the button. Now get that strike in."

"No chance Ichiro and Shackleton would have survived that, is there?" Salisbury asked as she skidded to a halt beside the ammo. White silk fluttered down around them as they smashed open the crates and filled their weapons, pockets, and webbing with as much as they could carry.

"What the fuck is that swarming up the valley?" Barnes said, voice crackling with interference. "It's like a thick red sea, flowing up against gravity and–" He fell silent as the squad turned and spread out to meet the maggots.

"And he's seen the... whatever the fuck that is down there," Gemmell said.

"The fuck is happening here?" Barnes yelled.

"Call in all the damn strike!" Jimenez ordered.

"It's Ichiro!" Salisbury said, pointing between the trees.

Shackleton was nowhere in sight, but Ichiro, battered and bloody, limped along some two hundred yards away. He paused, looked over his shoulder, and stopped.

"What's he doing?"

The man stood tall, saluted, then bowed low from the waist. Then he moved as quickly as his injuries would allow, laying a line of mines across the valley floor.

"Ichiro, no!" Salisbury yelled.

The crimson wave swelled up behind and Ichiro turned to face it. He lifted his arms to either side as it engulfed him, then the valley lit up with noise and fire again. Red meat sailed and sizzled, green blood sprayed.

The squad howled their rage and started crossfire containment again. The scream of the C-16 engines came directly overhead, Barnes flying back the way he'd come.

"We need support!" Jimenez yelled. "Did you make the call?"

"Cap, there's no time," Barnes said. "Even if you carve up this wave of whatever the fuck it is you're fighting, there'll be another one less than thirty minutes behind it. And again and again. And that hole in the fucking world is growing."

"That doesn't mean we quit, pilot! We might be a band of scumbag mercs, but we fight the bad guys, right? We have to hold this valley."

"Fall back!" Gemmell yelled, and he dragged an ammo crate with one hand while continuing to fire with the other. The squad matched his active retreat, bullets flying, tracers flashing.

"Exactly the point, Cap," Barnes said. "There's no way you'll contain this until help arrives unless those fuckers stop being born."

The C-16 screamed overhead again, once more heading down the valley.

"Barnes, the fuck are you doing?"

"Making good use of that unexpected gift from Honduras, Cap. Otherwise you guys will never make it out of there, and if you don't make it out, those fuckers will. Two-thousand pounds of C4 and all the rest, plus the mostly full fuel tanks of our bird here, should close that ugly hole, right?"

"Barnes, no!"

"You tell her I'm a fucking hero, Cap." Barnes's voice was tight with emotion. "Tell her at least we had Martinique. See you in Valhalla, you fucks!"

The C-16 engines howled a to a pitch Jimenez had never heard before, then a concussive wave rocked up the valley. Fire and smoke mushroomed up above trees then the shockwave hit them as the sound of the explosion blew the hearing out of their ears. The thunder of gunfire slowly came back as they kept up the fight against the advancing maggots.

"You mad bastard!" Jimenez yelled, and only hoped it had been enough. If that throat had indeed been blown back to wherever it came from, perhaps they had a chance. The crack and boom of falling rock echoed up to them as they fired in retreat, but still the carnivorous wave kept breaking. They had to stop it.

Gemmell dashed his hopes immediately. "We can't hold them back with just four of us, Cap!"

And the big man was right. Down to four, they couldn't cover enough ground and the maggots threatened to flank them.

"Fall back to the pass!" Jimenez said. "Grab whatever you can carry and run like fuck!"

They gathered what ammo they could and bolted.

"That rocky pass was only about sixty feet wide," Jimenez yelled as they sprinted. "It's high-sided and much easier to defend. If we can contain the maggots in this valley, and if Barnes has successfully prevented any more from coming, we have a chance."

"Every wave is bigger than the last," Haversham said.

"How big is this one? Did another get out behind it?"

"Who fucking cares? We fight until we can't any longer."

There was a scream behind and Jimenez turned to look. Shackleton had tripped, tree roots catching her feet as she had tried to run and carry a grenade case with her.

"Don't fucking stop!" she shouted, as the dark red tide mounted behind her, tumbling through the trees.

"On your feet, soldier!" Jimenez yelled.

Shackleton shook her head, gave him a smile that said it all. No time. She pulled a grenade pin with her teeth and hugged it and the box containing twenty more to her chest as she fell into the shadow of the advancing worms.

Jimenez stared. *I don't deserve these people. The world doesn't deserve them.* "Incoming!" he roared, and then the grenades went up.

The blast took Jimenez, Haversham, and Gemmell off their feet, the heat of it scorching their backs. The stench of cooking maggot filled the air as they scrambled back up to run on. Haversham yelped in pain. A chunk of tree wood, sharp and ragged, stuck sideways from his thigh. He couldn't stand.

Gemmell ran back, leaving the ammo crate he'd been dragging where it was, and got a hand under Haversham's arm. As he heaved up, Haversham shook him off. "Don't be a fool! You can't carry me and fight."

"Get up!" Gemmell shouted at him, but Jimenez saw the amount of blood coming from the leg wound. Haversham would bleed out, even if he could stand. They had no time for field dressings.

With a lump in his throat, Jimenez barked an order. "Gemmell, to me!"

The big man looked back, desperation in his eyes. Haversham nodded, then caught Jimenez's eye. "A fucking honor, Cap," he said.

"Fuck!" Gemmell grabbed up his crate again and ran back, leaving Haversham where he lay. The red tide was almost on him.

"Go! Stop them!" Haversham yelled at Jimenez and Gemmell, then turned and fired from the ground, sweeping full auto left and right into the surge of maggots as they came over the burning corpses of their brethren. One maggot scooped Haversham into its tooth-filled maw and still he fired, blowing it apart even as it tried to swallow him. As it flopped wet and dead over him, he tried to scramble back, but another worm, bigger than the first, swallowed the lot and Haversham vanished down its wet throat, his weapon still barking fire.

Jimenez's teeth threatened to crack apart, he clenched them so hard. His entire squad decimated, only he and Gemmell left. They had to stop this.

They reached the start of the narrow rocky pass that led down into the gorge and started to clamber up its steep incline.

"We need to get high enough to hold here," Jimenez said, gasping for breath as he scrambled up. The rock would bottleneck the worms. If they could only hold this ground, not let any maggots past... But four of them hadn't been enough down on the valley floor, so would two be enough even here? Regardless, they had no choice.

He sensed a lack of movement beside himself and paused, spun around. Gemmell was fifty yards back, scrabbling at a crack in the rock face. Sheer gray stone towered above him on either side.

"Get up here!" Jimenez yelled, the surge of thick red death was almost on Gemmell's back.

"You have to mop up the last of 'em, Cap!" Gemmell called up, and raised a detonator in one hand.

"Gemmell, no!"

"We've got to get them all, right?" Gemmell said, a grin on his wide face. "Like the fucking Pokemon."

Jimenez forced a smile and nodded. "Gotta catch 'em all!"

The thick tide of maggots rose up, forced atop one another in the rapidly narrowing pass, dropping Gemmell into their shadow. As Gemmell slammed his thumb down on the button, Jimenez turned and scrambled up the rocky slope.

The explosion knocked him down, sharp stones carving up his face and palms, but he crawled on. Deep, booming cracks echoed behind as the rock above the blown-out side split apart and fell in. Rock dust, smoke, fire and green blood roiled into the air as the low end of the pass became blocked by a new wall of fallen boulders.

Jimenez found a high point and turned, feet braced wide as the remaining maggots came boiling over the top of the rock wall blocking the low end of the pass. Clearly there were still enough pressed up against it that others tumbled over them like water filling a vessel, and flooded past the top edge. But Jimenez had the high ground and the way up was narrower than ever now. And he had a lot of ammo.

He lobbed grenades over, dozens of maggots at a time blown to smithereens, the wave falling briefly back before surging up and over again. Jimenez raked them with fire, moving forward as he went, sending the fat red bastards tumbling back down into the pass. In moments he was standing atop the newly made wall shooting down into a mass of red flesh and green ooze at anything that moved.

Captain Jimenez sat across from the sweating Cantrell, fury seething in his gut. "Well?" he asked.

"You did a fine job," Cantrell said.

"What does that mean? It hasn't come back?"

"Correct. You said you went back and could see no trace of the… the…"

"Let's call it the throat, shall we? Because honestly, who knows what the fuck it really was."

"The throat. Okay. Well, you're right. It seems your pilot's amazing sacrifice did sever its connection. There's nothing moving down there, no trace of the base or anything else. And the magnetic interference has ceased. Whatever you met down there, it's gone. You beat it."

"Beat it?" Jimenez asked, stunned at the man's audacity. "It very nearly beat us. They're all fucking dead, Cantrell!"

Cantrell held up both palms in a gesture of surrender. "I'm sorry. But so is everything else. We can't thank you enough."

Rage bubbled through Jimenez's veins. "You knew this was more than some rebels breaking into a lab to steal tech, didn't you?"

Cantrell licked his lips. "We suspected it might be more than–"

"They saved the fucking world!" he yelled. "And they will never be credited for it." He stood, leaned over the desk. "Fuck you!" And he punched Cantrell right in his smug face, sending the man backwards onto the floor, chair and all, howling in shock and pain. Jimenez pulled a pistol from his jacket and shot over the desk, right between Cantrell's eyes.

"I got a fucking pony to ride."

THE DEMON LOCKE

Originally published in SNAFU: Medivac, which was a charity volume of the series to raise money for cancer treatment for author James A. Moore. Jim is a great guy and a regular contributor to the SNAFU series, as well as the author of numerous novels and stories.

The Demon Locke

"You have got to be shitting me."

"The Demon Locke has protected humanity for centuries, Mr Clay."

"Sergeant Clay, please. Mr Clay was my father and I have not earned that title yet."

"As you wish, Sergeant. But regardless, I am not shitting you."

The woman, Sister Agatha, smiled softly, condescendingly Clay thought. In her long, plain grey dress, she looked kind of like a nun, but without a wimple of any sort. Her hair hung long and straight, ash blonde.

He shook his head, trying to decide whether maybe there was a hidden camera somewhere in the old castle. "Okay, let me get this straight. You have a Most Important Nun–"

"The Demon Locke, yes."

"Right. And she stops demons from getting out."

"Yes."

"But she's sick and we have to get her back down the mountain to the hospital you've had set up in the old school on the edge of town."

"Yes. You passed it on the way here, you were supposed to log its location."

"We did." Clay frowned. "But you really need the SAS to move one nun?"

Sister Agatha sighed. "I was told you'd simply follow orders."

"You are not my CO, lady. Explain it to me like I'm five. Why not just take her down in a damn wheelbarrow or something if it's that important?"

Sister Agatha interlaced her fingers and rested her chin on them for a moment in thought. "Let me give you an abridged version of the story," she said, looking up again. "Centuries ago, humanity came under attack from beings best described as demons."

"Like, demons from Hell?" Clay said. "You're telling me Hell is real?"

"Well, at the time, that's what they thought. These days we think maybe it's not so simple, and perhaps it's more like another dimension that interacts intermittently with our own, and these creatures are of that dimension. But let's say demons from Hell just for brevity's sake, yes?"

Clay inclined his head, gestured for her to continue.

"Very well. So, our Order was established with ancient knowledge, to find a way to banish these demons. There were various magical and occult options open to the ancient Sisters, and other groups helped them. It's a very complicated process, but in essence a system was developed. A person, The Demon Locke, is able to prevent these beings from getting into our dimension by closing all access into herself." Agatha pursed her lips a moment and Clay had impure thoughts, then felt slightly guilty. Then again, was she even a nun really?

"Imagine a powerful magnet," Sister Agatha said. "So strong, nothing can escape its pull. It gathers everything metal to it and holds it in place. The Sister who takes on the role of the Demon Locke fulfills a purpose like that, only she pulls to herself and holds onto all the possible connections between our dimension and the other. Hell, if you will. So all the time the Demon Locke is in place, the demons can't get through."

"Hence the name."

"Correct, Sergeant. Hence the name. Now, that's obviously a very dangerous position to put one person in, so they have to be protected. This castle is that protection. The rest of us keep the castle secure with powerful wards, the Demon Locke remains safe, and she keeps the demons from invading our world. That's why the castle is so remote. But now that very remoteness is causing a problem, as the Demon Locke is sick and requires immediate medical attention."

Sergeant Clay nodded, thinking. "Okay, assuming I buy all this Halloween shit, let me ask a couple of questions."

"If they're quick."

"Right. Okay, one: Why isn't there another Locke woman? Seems dangerous to only have one."

"Indeed. As soon as the new Locke is appointed, she begins training her apprentice. Usually there are decades, and it only take a few years to train the successor. But our current Locke is young, and unexpectedly sick. The apprentice is not yet ready."

Clay nodded. "Something to think about there, huh? Maybe train up a few at a time?"

Sister Agatha sighed again. "In fourteen hundred years this has never happened." She held up a hand as Clay opened his mouth to speak. "But yes, your observation is erudite."

"Is it now? I've never been called that before. Okay, second question: Why don't you bring the medics here?"

"A fair question. Do you see any power outlets in these stone walls, Sergeant?"

"You know there are generators and shit? Or run a power line up here?"

"Of course, but for fourteen hundred years we've been self-sufficient. And a generator isn't stable enough. The Demon Locke has reached a point where she requires daily dialysis. That is not possible here. We have organised everything in the old school, just six miles from the foot of our mountain, where there's a stable power supply, doctors on hand, medicine, and so on. We need your help to get her down the mountain, and along six miles of road to that location. There we have set up the wards like the ones here and once she's inside all will be well. It's moving her that's the problem. We can't maintain moving protections. From when we leave these walls until we get her inside the school, the demons will try to get her. That's where you come in."

"They won't just run rampant, these demons?"

"We don't think so. Their priority will be to kill the Locke, thereby freeing themselves more permanently."

Clay sniffed, sucked his teeth. "This is the most mental medevac I've ever heard of."

"Nevertheless, here we are."

"We have to fight off demons?"

"Yes. They will manifest in any way they can. Once we

move the Locke and her power is interrupted, they will come. They will manifest near her, as she will be able to hold some degree of control, but not enough to keep them out entirely. And we cannot protect her while she's moving."

"A shame we can't get out Land Rovers up through all these trees. The path down is pretty narrow. You planning to carry her?"

"We have a plan to mover her."

Clay nodded. "You know, in the SAS we have a saying. Kiss."

Agatha frowned.

"It's an acronym. Keep it simple, stupid. Would it be fair to say that the simplest interpretation of this medevac is for my men to travel with you lot to the new location and kill anything that comes near us along the way?"

Sister Agatha smiled. "Yes, Sergeant Clay. That would be perfect."

"Okay, you grunts, listen up. We have about two miles of winding path through this forest, back the way we came, until we reach the foot of the mountain. At the base will apparently be a truck, where we left our Land Rovers. We and that truck will drive six miles to our target location. The Sisters will be travelling in that wagon." Clay pointed to the long, narrow canvas-covered wooden wagon in the castle courtyard. "We stay in formation around it and murder with great prejudice anything that comes near. And I mean anything. Even a fucking ant. Any questions?"

Corporal Patel raised his hand.

"Yes?"

"Why not horses?" Patel's face was scrunched in a mixture of discomfort and disgust.

Clay looked at his seven Operators, saw variations of the same expression on each of their faces. He had decided not to ask, but now the subject had been brought up, he couldn't ignore it. He should have known better than to ask them for questions.

He turned back to the wagon, standing before the closed wooden gates, and realised his own face had twisted to match Patel's. The Demon Locke, her apprentice, and Sister Agatha were inside, hidden by the canvas sides. In front, where there really should be horses, six more Sisters stood in two lines of three, leather harnesses jury-rigged to fit around their torsos. They leaned gently into their harnesses, ready to haul the wagon along. Clay hoped they were fit nuns – two miles was a long pull. Then again, it was all downhill, zigzagging along the well-trodden dirt path between the trees. The six women returned his gaze with unself-conscious equanimity.

"Why not horses?" Sergeant Clay called out.

Sister Agatha poked her head out of the canvas flaps at the front of the wagon. "Because the demons will manifest through any living thing. A horse, a bird, anything. The only thing they cannot subsume is a human being, as our minds are too strong. Normally one horse would pull this narrow wagon up the mountain when we re-supply in town. We thought six Sisters would probably account for one horse."

"Demons, Sergeant?" Patel asked.

Enough of this. Fuck all the nonsense, the essence of this job was simple. "No more questions, squad. These crazy ladies are going to run a wagon down to a truck, we kill any beast that comes near." He frowned. "Got it?"

"Yes, Sergeant!" they yelled in unison.

He looked over the group. Two patrols. Half a troop. Eight soldiers including himself. He had a wave of concern, suddenly wondering if they would be enough. Demons? Really? They didn't even have their captain here and Clay wondered if command had seriously underestimated the importance of this mission. Had Clay and his men been sent purely to humour some crazy religious order? What if all this was real? But it was too late to do anything about that now.

They all carried C8 Carbines with plenty of spare ammo, and each had a Sig Sauer P226. Between them there were a bunch of Flash-Bangs and a decent supply of L109A1 HE

Fragmentation Grenades hanging in their webbing. Despite that, Clay suddenly felt decidedly underdressed. A two-mile run and a six-mile drive. It would have to be enough.

"Patel, Farley, over to the left side of the wagon and stay there the whole way," he shouted. "Dillbury and Canton, you take the right side. East and Stephenson hold the rear. Brown, you're with me in front."

The group ran to their positions, immediately tensed and ready, carbines held at port arms.

"We're ready when you are," Clay called out.

"We've been ready for some time," Sister Agatha said, poking her head out again. She looked up to two sisters at the gate. "Let's go!"

Those sisters each pulled hard and opened both sides of the gate. The six women in the harnesses strained forward and the wagon creaked, then began to roll. The soldiers jogged alongside, holding their positions, eyes everywhere. A more bizarre assignment Clay could not imagine, but it all sank away in favour of training. The path up the remote Scottish mountain was familiar to them, having hiked it earlier in the day. It wound its way down to a gravelly area of level ground where the truck would apparently be waiting. Two Land Rovers were already there, having brought Clay and his men that far. They would use the Rovers to escort the truck the last bit along the road. Simple, right?

He glanced back to six nuns driving their shoulders into harnesses, legs pumping under their flowing grey habits, and shook his head. There was nothing simple about any of this.

They cleared the gates and started along the hard-packed earth of the mountain path. Another perimeter fence surrounded the entire castle, signs on the outside that read *Private Property – Keep Out*. Clay and his men had let themselves in there that morning and left the gate open. Within moments they were bearing down on it but Sister Agatha's voice cut through Clay's thoughts.

"It begins!"

He glanced back and saw her pointing up ahead of them. Turning back he jumped to see the sky filled with birds, a dark cloud of crows swooping in over the treetops.

"Kill every fucking bird!" he yelled and lifted his weapon.

Eight carbines burst into life and the sight was hard to believe. As they raked fire through the flock, the birds burst into flames when hit, spiralling down like WW2 Spitfires. They began to shriek and wail, a sound unlike anything he'd ever heard from a crow before. Unlike anything he'd heard from any creature.

The birds wheeled to the left, went up and away, and Clay was about to relax when they came back around, diving once more. This time they seemed to flex and pulse in the air, growing exponentially larger, stretching the frames of their bodies. Feathers burst free, but they flew on. The troop began firing again and the swollen, twisted avians exploded in fire and smoke, filling the air with their flames and their screams.

Then one broke through. Clay tried to track it as it came low over the nuns in the harness.

"Beware crossfire!" he yelled, then the bird struck the centre nun on the left full in the face.

She wailed and staggered, blood flooding her face. For a moment she stumbled and was dragged by her harness, then with an incredible show of strength, she found her feet and ran on. Farley ran wide as the crow that had attacked her came around and he crouched low to shoot up at it and not risk hitting any of the nuns or soldiers. The crow exploded, a stink of sulphur and something far less pleasant. Fire rained down from it and two nuns beat furiously at their hair to put out the embers and the wagon rolled on.

"What the fuck is this?" Stephenson shouted from the rear of the group.

"A job," Clay called back. "It's a deployment like any other. Don't sweat the details, kill everything!"

"Two o'clock!" Canton called and all eyes turned.

"Again," Clay muttered under his breath. "You have to be shitting me."

Dozens of red deer came galloping through the trees. Some with huge antlers, some without, but all with bright red, fiery eyes. Their maws split in howls to reveal unnatural rows of sharp white fangs. As they drew nearer, their spines arched, shoulders popped out in grotesque slabs of muscles. They grew and stretched to the size of cattle, but the eight soldiers were already firing.

Clay pulled a grenade free and lobbed it past the front wave with all his might. It fell just behind the advancing herd, red fur and bloody meat spraying up into the air along with dirt and grass and leaves.

Where bullets struck the demon deer, blood poured out thick and black. Flames licked back from their faces, those burning eyes singeing the fur of their heads to charcoal. As they fell under the heavy ordnance, some stumbled and went own, others leaped and bounded with the speed and grace of savannah gazelles. Except these were now the size of shire horses.

If the screams of the crows had been disturbing, the howls emanating from these beasts was truly disarming. The sounds turned Clay's blood to ice, made his stomach roil and his knees weak.

"This side too!" East roared as the first herd drew near and Clay glanced back to see more Hell-deer catching up behind the wagon. East and Stephenson ran backwards, raking fire as they went. They would have to manage. Patel dropped back a little from the other side to assist them, Farley moving forward of the wagon to fire across and assist Clay and Brown.

Clay looked at Brown's face and saw the man's eyes stretch wide. He turned back to the front in time to see the foremost giant deer was upon them. He went full-auto at point-blank range, shredding the beast's shoulder and ribs, but not before it had Brown by the face in its fang-filled maw. The soldier screamed as he was lifted off his feet and carried away.

Clay turned, still firing, and finally the beast stumbled and went down, rolling over Brown as it did so. The soldier's body was jelly as it was crushed and flipped. He landed beside the dead deer, his face gone, just red mince from the base of his neck up.

The wagon rolled on.

A nun screamed as another deer got close. Clay and

Farley emptied cartridges into it from either side, but it got to the front right nun first. It grabbed at her shoulder, shaking its head like a crazed dog, ripping her arm free. The nun shrieked, blood geysering from the hole where her arm had been. Their bullets took the deer down and it thankfully fell to one side, the nuns managing to haul the wagon to the right just in time to avoid crashing over its carcass.

The one who had lost her arm stumbled, face white as marble, and fell. Hanging in the harness, she was dragged along, feet bouncing behind, her habit billowing like a windsock. The woman on her left, in the other front harness, reached across with a face set in determination, and yanked at a leather strap. The dead nun fell from the released harness, the two behind jumped her as she rolled, then the wagon wheels *bump-bumped* over her body and she was left broken and bloodied on the trail.

Clay looked over to the middle row, to the nun who'd lost an eye. The front of her habit was dark with blood, her face pale where it wasn't scarlet, but she ran on, teeth gritted in a snarl of effort. He shook his head. These women were something else.

"The truck!" someone yelled, maybe Farley.

Clay looked up, relieved to see the trees opening out and the gravelly ground ahead. Their two Land Rovers stood side by side where they'd left them. Not far away, a 7-tonne box-back truck waited, the roller door at the rear open. Clay saw two nuns in there waiting, a third leaning out of the driver's window, brows tight in concern.

The nuns in the harnesses turned sideways and got the wagon as close to the back of the truck as they could. They yanked on their quick release straps and ran to the side of the wagon. All except the one who had lost an eye. She collapsed, waving her compatriots on.

Sister Agatha threw aside the canvas covering. She and the apprentice in there with her lifted a third, looking weak and thin, her face grey as ash. The Locke, Clay presumed. With care, but speed, they hefted the sick woman and jumped clear across from the wagon to the truck. Had they practiced that manoeuvre? The women who had run with the wagon clambered in behind.

"You are shitting me!" Dillbury said.

Clay turned to look and saw a flock of giant, swollen sheep hammering across the heath. They looked like storm clouds rolling along the ground, but for their black faces and rage-red eyes. Each the size of a car, legs grotesquely swollen, their bleats echoed with ear-piercing ferocity.

The soldiers lobbed grenades and fired in sweeping, controlled bursts, exploding the first wave in sulphurous flames.

"Get to the Rovers!" Clay yelled. "I'm in front, Canton in behind the truck!"

Before the demon sheep could get too close, the soldiers ran for the Land Rovers. The roller door on the back of the truck banged closed and the truck roared, wheel-spinning as the nun driving it peeled out.

Clay leaped into the driver's seat of his Land Rover, trusting Patel and Farley to get in and start firing. He was immediately deafened by their carbines and knew they were on it. Brown should be there too, but his corpse was crushed back in the forest.

Canton would be in the driver's seat of the other Land Rover, Dillbury, East, and Stephenson riding with him. Clay accelerated hard past the truck, saw the driving nun's teeth bared in determination as she hunched over the wheel. He pulled in front of her and matched speed, saw sheep all around exploding in bursts of sulphurous flame from his men's bullets. Their bleats were piercing screams that tore at his eardrums even over the almost continuous gunfire.

"In front!" he yelled, appalled at the sudden appearance of some fifty demonic, over-sized sheep blocking the road. Why the fuck did Scotland have to have so many godsdamned sheep?

In the rearview mirror he saw Patel stand up through the open top of the Land Rover, an M72 LAW compact anti-tank rocket launcher resting on his shoulder. Clay smiled as the rocket whooshed over the Land Rover's cab and sent demon flesh and wool up in a billowing cloud. Taking no chances, Patel reloaded and fired again. The Land Rover shot into the swirling smoke, bouncing over pieces of sheep and broken road. Through the roiling haze, Clay watched in the rearview and let go a sigh of relief when the nun's truck burst through, jouncing crazily, but still heading fundamentally straight ahead.

The journey stretched into a surreal mayhem of continuous assault. Canton would frequently pull up alongside, East matching Patel with his own M72 LAW, blowing flocks of Hell-sheep into the dark beyond. The others kept up a furious rate of fire, taking out any beasts that got near.

At the five-mile mark, another flock of fiery birds came in, tried to assault the group from above. Most were shot, some managed to hit the truck, but even in their swollen state they didn't have the power to get through the hard metal shell of the truck's box.

We're gonna make it. Then Clay cursed himself for jinxing the operation.

From the right side, about one o'clock, the heath was churned into dust by a herd of Highland Cows, their long red fur streaming in the wind as they ran, curving horns grown to ridiculous proportions. They came at a furious pace, on a direct collision course with the truck. Demonically expanded to the size of small trucks themselves, there was no way the nuns would survive that impact.

As they barrelled along the small country road at close to eighty miles per hour, Clay desperately tried to think of a plan. How did anyone stop something like that? Then he saw Canton's Land Rover coming up beside the nun's truck. Staying in front, letting Patel and Farley keep the road ahead clear of sheep, he watched as Dillbury, East, and Stephenson clambered up from the Land Rover and jumped onto the roof of the speeding truck. They held on for dear life as Canton swerved the Land Rover to the right, putting it directly between the truck and the stampeding Highland cattle.

"You mad fucking bastard!" Clay cried with glee as he saw the flames licking out of the back of the Land Rover. The amount of ammo, grenades and rockets in that vehicle made it a bomb of significant proportions.

"Get clear you fucker!" Clay yelled at Canton, who was clearly too far away to hear a thing, especially over the roar of engines and the barrage of gunfire. Sheep exploded in front of Clay, but he largely ignored them when he saw Canton launch himself out of the speeding Land Rover. The lunatic flew backwards and managed to lob a grenade back into the vehicle, then he hit the heather and rolled crazily. The Land Rover reached a few metres in front of the Highland cows, and went up in a burst of light and an ear-splitting explosion that sucked away all other sound. Red fur flew, long, curing horns span up into the air. Other cattle around the edges of the racing herd were blown off their feet sideways, still more pitched into the crater made by the exploding vehicle.

With a whoop of joy he couldn't hear, Clay roared on, the nun's truck tight on his arse, and they saw the large building ahead that had been converted ready for the Demon Locke. It was surrounded by a chain link fence, two nuns standing ready at the gate.

"How many of these bloody women are there?" Clay wondered aloud, as they hauled the gates open and he drove straight in, the truck right behind. They skidded to a halt and the roller door of the truck went up.

"Get her inside," Sister Agatha said. "You know what to do, the doctors are waiting."

Clay climbed out of the Land Rover as his men jumped off the roof of the truck. He walked up to Agatha, but she ignored him, watching the skies, the land outside the compound. She frowned as a huge cloud descended from the north. A cloud of birds, Clay realised, oversized and grotesque, bearing down on the building. Sister Agatha pursed her lips, Clay saw her hands tighten into fists.

"We're safe in here, right?" Clay asked.

"We're inside the wards, yes. But if they can't get in here, they'll go elsewhere while they can."

The neat formation of birds suddenly stuttered and fractured. Some tumbled from the air, others twisted and shrank, then flew off in random directions.

Sister Agatha smiled. "The Locke is in place," she said

quietly. "She's okay." She turned and walked into the building.

Clay followed her, immediately assailed by the smells of a hospital. The small, pale woman from the wagon was the centre of fervent activity, doctors and nurses moving busily around her. She leaned sideways to see Clay and smiled.

"Sergeant," she said, her voice weak, strained, but her eyes glittered with alertness. "Thank you."

Clay nodded. She seemed anything but the single human being holding hordes of demons at bay. "You're okay?" he asked.

She smiled so sadly that it cleaved his heart a little. "No, not really. But I'll live long enough now to ensure the safety of the world. And maybe a little longer, if I'm lucky."

"You're..." Clay paused, pursed his lips. "You're doing it now? Stopping the demons?"

"Yes. It's a state of being, Sergeant Clay. It's complicated." She smiled again, more good-naturedly this time. "I know I make it look easy. It's not, but I do my best."

"We'll leave you to rest," Sister Agatha said. She gently put a hand to Clay's arm, guided him back outside. As they emerged into the warm, fresh air, she turned to him and smiled genuinely for the first time. Her face softened with it, kind and friendly. "Thank you, Sergeant. And I'm sorry for your loss."

"You too. And you're welcome. We're all done here?"

"Yes, you saved the world today, Sergeant. You and your men."

"All in a day's work."

"And while we're here, we'll train more than one apprentice." Sister Agatha gave another smile and squeezed Clay's shoulder, then turned and went back inside.

"Hey," came a voice from outside the fence.

Clay turned and saw Canton, bruised and bloody, heather stuck in his webbing.

"Who wants burgers for dinner?" Canton asked, pulling grass from between his teeth.

AND FIRE POURED FORTH

This is an original story, never before published.

And Fire Poured Forth

"Still nothing, Colonel," Dabrowska said, folding her antenna, slinging her pack.

Colonel Hardy sniffed. "So we've lost contact with everyone. Well, we still have a mission. We extract these scientists and get back to base."

Scientists, Aker thought. What can they do about all this?

The first time the earth split open and magma poured out like pus from an infected wound, the news cycle was almost amused by it. Something different to the political bullshit saturating the airwaves. Ha ha, motherfucker, who's laughing now?

"Corporal Aker, are you dreaming about big tits again?"

Aker jumped, then noticed everyone else was standing up, ready to move out. Scrambling to his feet he shouldered his pack and weapon. "Always dreaming about big tits, Colonel."

"You're the biggest tit here, Aker," Gunnell said, smirking.

Aker shrugged, gave her a wink.

Sniggers rippled through the squad. Eight men and women, trained to be the best of the best. Utterly useless in the face of all this.

When ruptures began appearing more rapidly, all around the world, people got scared. Apocalypse junkies rejoiced, the planet was shaking us off. Then a rupture split downtown Manhattan from end to end in less than three minutes and thousands fell screaming into molten rock. That was the final straw. Society crumbled like old cake.

"Move out," Colonel Hardy barked. "Stay tight, stay alert."

The squad trudged forward, nerves taut.

Despite the breakdown of civilisation, humanity fought to survive. Wait it out, the scientists said. Some unprecedented effect, almost certainly gravitational. Then the first demons clambered out of the molten, fiery fissures and everyone knew it was the end of the world.

Colonel Hardy pointed up the rocky ridge, sunlight reflecting off the sweaty dark skin of his thickly-muscled arm. "The target is one click that way and we can only hope they have supplies there." His Jamaican accent always calmed Aker. "Hopefully a good number of soldiers too. We've lost contact, but I choose to believe that's a problem with the satellites and not a personnel issue."

They'd survived a couple of months already, helping civilians where they found them, fighting off demons where they could, retreating often. Maybe they could make it a few months more. Anecdotal evidence suggested the appearance of new ruptures was slowing down, but with the thousands already open the planet was a minefield of fire. Hell on earth. And if the demons didn't stop coming out, surely humanity was finished.

"Did you hear something?" Gray asked, eyes flicking left and right. The kid was too highly strung by far, he put Aker on edge.

"Only your yammering," Hardy said. "Keep it down."

They were in rough terrain, a huge rupture about a half-mile across smouldered far to the west. The remote base they headed for was the only mark of civilization for miles around and still out of sight behind sharp and tumbled rock.

"Single file!" Colonel Hardy strode on, weapon held forward-ready. Sergeant Mark Summers pulled Aker closer as they followed, the Privates all falling in place behind them.

"Corporal," he whispered, voice masked by the crunching of boots on the gravelly ground. "You think Gray is all right?"

Aker shrugged. "He's not coping well. About ready to snap, you think?"

Summers dragged a hand back over sandy hair. "Was gonna ask you the same thing. I don't want to risk the others if he cracks."

"I don't think that's the way he'd go. If he goes."

"Watch him. Don't let him become a liability."

Aker swallowed a shudder, nodded to show he

understood. There was a high price to being the sniper sometimes, especially when your Sergeant suggested you shoot a squad mate, which is exactly what Summers meant. Gray was a twenty-two year old private with next to no experience and he was fraying like old sackcloth. In truth, perhaps his was the only sane response to the end of the world. But Aker refused to give in. They were warriors. They go down fighting and not before. He thought Gray was more likely to quit and eat his own barrel than become a liability, but would wait and see. Sergeant Summers gave him a slap on the shoulder and hustled up next to Colonel Hardy. They conversed in low tones.

Gray was a newbie grunt who'd found himself lucky to survive the last encounter. Aker grimaced. Man, that was a shitfight. Twenty of them sent to find the scientists who claimed to know what was happening, and they were down to eight. Low on ammo and supplies. What a mess. But seven of us are good soldiers, Aker thought grimly.

Private Jen Gunnell followed him, her long hair tied back, face half-smiling. She was always ready to joke about something. She talked quietly to Private Adrian Shotbolt, stoic, but funny as fuck if you paid attention. Humour drier than a camel's balls. No wonder he and Gunnell got along. Private Harold James, the serious Nigerian, quietly followed them, head down. He looked up as Private Helena Dabrowska moved alongside. The young Pole gave him a soft smile. He nodded back, tight, guarded.

And then Private Ollie Gray hurrying along at their six, eyes everywhere. Tall, skinny, horse-faced son-of-a-bitch, looking around like he was hunting for an exit. Might be a favour to them all if he deserted. But Aker would give him a chance to find his fight.

They'd passed through a city the day before. The demons had left it a charred, broken, empty ghost town. A rupture half a mile long belching and glowing right up the central business district. It was too hot to get closer than a hundred metres out, but it didn't seem to be birthing any more demons. At least, not right then. Skyscrapers fallen like old trees laid half in and half out of the incandescent wound in the ground, the stone and steel of their construction melting and dripping like wax. If anyone was alive back there, they were hiding well, even from soldiers passing through. Can't blame them, Aker thought. Then they ran into more demons, lost more personnel, lost their vehicles.

But Colonel Hardy wanted to keep moving, crawl if they had to, liberating anyone along the way until they achieved their objective or died trying. Aker couldn't help wondering if it was all for nothing. Unless the ruptures *had* stopped. Unless the demons *were* finite in number. Maybe then, with enough others acting like they were, they might be able to take the planet back. There had to be other squads, other military, still going. Maybe the boffins could repair communications, help them learn what was happening elsewhere in the country, in the world. Coordinate a proper fight. He had to believe the threat was beatable. The alternative was horrendous.

Heat haze over the next ridge of rock caught his eye. Simultaneously, Hardy yelled, "Incoming!" and his assault rifle barked alive.

Summers dropped to one knee beside the Colonel, his own weapon bucking with fire and noise, his face grim. The rest of squad ran to fan out alongside them. Experience had taught that holding a line and delivering heavy ordnance was the best defence.

Aker ran aside fifty metres or so and hit the dirt, the support struts of his L121A1 anti-materiel rifle swinging down. He would never get used to seeing the fuckers pouring over the landscape. Demons. Is that really what they were? Some people early on speculated they were aliens, but they came out of the ground. Best not to think about it, Aker decided. Just shoot them. They go down, at least. Eventually.

It was a swarm of the bastards. Ape-like bodies wreathed in fire, sentient furnaces lumbering along. Over-long arms swinging in counter-balance to short, thick legs. Literal living flame, roaring and howling, incinerating everything they touched. They were huge, the smallest of them over seven feet tall. They grabbed a person, crushed them in a fiery embrace and then dropped the smouldering corpse and moved on. They had no purpose but mindless slaughter. Aker saw no reason for their existence except the pure punishment of humanity. He'd never been a religious man, but couldn't think of any other explanation for their situation than some Biblical Revelation.

A burning, wide-mouthed face lined up in his Schmidt & Bender sight and he put a 50 cal round through it. The head disintegrated in an explosion of fire and shards like glass or diamond, but he didn't have time to watch, to try to figure out what these things really were. As that one dropped, he turned his weapon for the next. His sight selected head after head and five went down before he had to pause, swap out the box for his next five rounds.

The squad had fanned out further, assault rifles thundering, a wide line turning to an arc to pen the demons in and take them down. But there were dozens of them, they just kept coming. They were slow at least. Aker had to stay back, watch for any breaking to flank or get too close, and pick them off. The fuckers looked and acted mindless, but they'd seen them cooperate, use strategy.

He kept half an eye on Gray, but the kid was pulling his weight even if his face was twisted into a mask of panic. His fire was wild and reckless, but only towards the demons. And then Gunnell was screaming, her eyes wide as she scrabbled at her webbing. She was out of ammo, the rest of the squad spread too wide to pass her more.

Her rifle hit the dirt and she pulled got two Glock 17s, one in each hand, pumping round after round, but 9mm wasn't enough to stop the things. They sensed her weakness, smart enough to see an opening. Hardy yelled for Shotbolt, next along, to give her support and he ran, assault rifle hammering. But the demons made ground. Aker took out one after another, but his fire rate was slow. Shotbolt was still thirty metres away when Gunnell's howls of fury turned into wails of pain. Her skin blistered, her fatigues blackened and smouldered as the demons got within a few metres, their radiant heat killing her. And then they had her, surrounding her in consuming fire. Her screams were silenced and the squad roared, in voice and weapon.

The demons broke the line, tried to circle the rest of the squad, hem them in. Aker was the only one outside their assault, picking them off one by one, but not quickly enough. Shotbolt was too close, frantically backpedalling as he raked short bursts left and right. His pale face whiter than chalk, his mouth wide in a cry Aker couldn't hear over the roar of weapons and demon fire. Shotbolt went up like a candle, just ignited even as he ran backwards. He managed to blow two demons back to hell as he burned, then they grabbed him and he was gone.

Aker swapped out ammo again, his mind whirling, *Fuck, fuck, fuck, this is bad.* Through a red veil of fury he swapped out clip after clip, dropping demons everywhere he saw them, all semblance of order gone, all strategy lost in the maelstrom of sheer panic.

And then there were piles of burning corpses littering the rocky ground, but no movement.

Gasping, heart racing, Aker rose to one knee. Hardy, Summers, James, Dabrowska and Gray were in a tight knot, facing out in all directions, all five of them looking left and right, scanning for any further threat. They were surrounded by the flaming corpses of dropped demons.

They'd got them all.

It was hard to believe. Hardy had angry blisters up his left arm, the shoulder of his fatigues charred and smoking. Dabrowska's hair, usually shoulder length and tied in a short ponytail, was almost gone, her face blackened on one side. They all winced at the heat surrounding them and then Hardy said something and they moved away from the carnage, heading back up the slope towards Aker. When they were all back together, in silence, they checked and dressed each other's burns and wounds.

Eventually Colonel Hardy stood up and shrugged his gear into place. His bandaged arm was stark white against the world, the only clean thing for miles around. "We keep going," he said, and walked away.

Two more damn fine soldiers just fell, Aker thought. We won't forget them. We will mourn them by fighting on.

They fell in behind Hardy and before long the base was

visible up ahead, a line of chain link against the grey rock. Office blocks, barracks, warehousing, all came into view as they got close. But no movement, no personnel. Vehicles abandoned, the whole place a tableau of loss. And lots of smoke.

"The fuck is the point, man?" Gray blurted. Tears marked tracks through the soot and dirt of his cheeks. "It's over, man. It's all fucking over!"

Hardy turned and walked back to Gray, his face expressionless. One meaty hand whipped out, cracked into Gray's jaw and sat the tall, skinny private on his arse. As Gray cradled his chin, lip already puffed and bleeding, Hardy turned away, continued on towards the base. The rest followed.

Aker crouched beside the young man. "You can stay there if you like. But nothing is over until you're dead. You want me to shoot you? Or you want to keep fighting?"

Gray looked up, tears running unabashed over his cheeks. He shook his head.

"All we can do is fight," Aker told him. "While there are people still alive, we fight. What else is there?"

He walked away and after a moment heard the scuffling of rock as Gray scurried to catch up. Poor bastard, Aker thought. He's really not cut out for this. Barely out of basic training and straight into the apocalypse.

They made their way to the base, eyes wide for threat, for movement. For anything. Columns of smoke rose lazily into the bright blue sky, one particularly thick and black from somewhere back and centre. It quickly became apparent the demons had been right through, maybe from the rupture to the west. The burning damage was everywhere, blackened vehicles and buildings, waxy dark patches on the concrete that used to be people, consumed by fire until only their stain remained. A lot of personnel, all gone.

"I'm guessing that swarm we just ran into were the leftovers from this fight," Hardy said.

Numerous demon corpses littered the ground among the buildings, glassy slag all that was left of whatever they were really made of, their flames gone out. When Aker kicked the remains, they shattered into shards and dust.

"You think we got 'em all, Colonel?" Summers asked.

Hardy nodded slowly. "Looks like. We were lucky, these guys did most of the work for us, but didn't quite manage to contain the swarm. We got the last few."

"Shame we didn't get here earlier," James said. "We might have been enough to tip the balance."

"Or we might have died with them, trapped in here." Dabrowska's frown was pure frustration.

"No use worrying about what ifs, soldiers." Hardy headed across the compound. "Stores and munitions this way. Let's stock up."

New disappointment wasn't long coming when they found the stores already stripped almost clean. What they carried was all they had, and it wasn't much. Gray picked up a couple of land mines, eyebrows raised at Hardy.

The Colonel shrugged, shook his head. "Where you gonna deploy those? Unnecessary weight."

They all grabbed extra Glock 17s and ammo, but they were pretty useless against the enemy. Pistols to a demon fight was the new knife to a gun fight.

"Look," Dabrowska said, pointing.

Three large green cylinders, strapped up and locked in a toughened cage, stood on a shelf.

"Tactical nukes," James said quietly. "The fuck were they expecting here?"

"Best not to think about any protocols they may have been considering," Hardy said. "Not our business."

He left the munitions facility, pointed to the right, where the thickest smoke roiled and twisted upwards. "The command centre is that way." Then he pointed left. "According to the little intel I have, the science research centre is over there. Sergeant Summers, take Gray and Dabrowska, check out command. Look for survivors, find comms, see if you can reach anyone. Aker and James, you're with me. Everyone keep an eye out for more stores or armoury, but I doubt we'll find any. I guess that's why they lost this fight. Shot 'emselves dry. Must've been hundreds of fucking demons."

Hardy headed towards the science station and without a word they all followed his orders. After a couple of minutes, Aker's radio crackled.

"This is Summers, copy."

He thumbed the handset. "We hear you, Sergeant."

"Nothing here. It's a slag pile. Looks like the personnel tried to group together and hold command but didn't survive long. Some big explosives were deployed, is my guess. That black smoke we saw coming in? It's basically everything of interest on fire over here. We can't even get close."

Hardy sighed. "Bring 'em back."

"Yes, sir. Sergeant, the Colonel says to regroup."

"On our way."

As they moved on together again through the research centre, the devastation was clear. Smouldering bodies, human and demon, lined the corridors, spot fires burning walls and furniture. Twice they retraced their steps, wondering if any part of the centre remained intact. They entered the largest building of the complex and spread out across a corridor marred by scorch marks and corpses. Smoke roiled lazily around the ceiling and they moved in a crouch to stay under it.

"I saw something!" Gray's voice was thin and high. He pointed his weapon to the left, panning it back and forth, his entire body trembling.

They dropped into defensive postures, grouped and ready. Gunnell's and Shotbolt's deaths still too fresh, all on edge. No one was ready for another fight. Maybe ever again.

The corridor widened out and something moved in the smoke.

"Back up," Hardy said. "We need to conserve ammo, so let's not run into a melee until we..."

A cry echoed out, muffled by distance. Human, male, and desperate. They froze. Slowly Aker raised his weapon, used his sight to see along the corridor. The smoke was thick in places, but patchy, and he saw brightness beyond it. The brightness of fire. Moving.

"Demons that way," he said quietly. Then his scope caught a glint of glass, and beyond that a pale, terrified face under a shock of red hair. "And people." At least one other person was moving behind the red-haired man.

He took a moment to properly assess the situation, then said, "Two or three people trapped behind blast doors. Four or five demons, maybe more, pinning them in. Looks like the demons can't get in, but I guess the people can't get out."

"Our scientists, maybe," Hardy said. "Can you take out the demons?"

"I can start, but they might get here faster than I can drop them all."

Hardy sniffed. "Okay. Get ready, people. Wait for Aker and we mop up the rest."

Aker laid down at the corner of the corridor and set up. It was only about a hundred metres, so the shots would be fairly easy. But bolt action and aim time gave him maybe three seconds between rounds at best, not accounting for smoke. He took slow breaths, watched through the scope for gaps in the haze and lined up on a glowing head. He ignored the red-haired fellow, staring hard through the extra-toughened glass, hope in his eyes.

"Game on," Aker said quietly and fired.

The report was huge and the head exploded in Aker's reticule but he was already retargeting. The next head blew and the demons turned, lumbering along the corridor towards them. Smoke roiled, blocked his vision and Aker had to reselect targets. He managed to track and drop a third then a fourth, then they were too close for the sight to cope and he was up, stumbling backwards as the squad engaged, rapid fire thundering in the tight space. But the end of the corridor came alive with fire and light. The last of the original demons dropped, but more were coming, five, six, seven, ten.

Using the sight over Hardy's shoulder, vibrating as the Colonel fired furiously left and right, the added light of their fire showed Aker a tumbled down wall the smoke had obscured before. Demons poured through the gap.

"Wall breach right by the doors!" His voice was high with panic. They didn't have the ammo for this. "Multiple incoming."

Dabrowska's rifle clicked empty and she double-handed

Glocks. Too much like Gunnell's last moments, so recent. The corridor ahead was full of fiery demons. Aker bucked from the shots he took standing, arms burning with the fifteen kilo weight of his weapon, swapping out boxes as fast as he could. Then Gray's rifle was empty too. The corridor thick with demons less than a hundred metres away.

Dabrowska dropped her Glocks and grabbed grenades from her webbing. "Fire in the hole!"

She lobbed them and the double blast wave pushed them back. The corridor was still standing, but it filled with flame. Smoke thickened the air. The fire bulged and pushed out as the demons forced their way past the corpses of their fellows.

"Fall back!" Hardy yelled, swapping in a new clip. It had to be his last. "We can't seal that breach!"

Gray suddenly let out a scream like a banshee. "Cover me!" And then he was sprinting down the hall, directly for the demons.

"What the fuck?" Hardy yelled, but they were all moving, getting cross positions to do what they could to protect Gray.

As he barrelled into the smoke he held up a landmine. Through his scope Aker saw two more jammed in his webbing. Crazy bastard took some after all. He wailed, his skin bubbling, hair smouldering away like touchpaper as he ducked and leaped between demons and the fiery lumps of their dead. The heat back there had to be intense. Aker watched him staggering and howling, the skin of his face blackened and mostly gone, then he dropped the mine right in the wall breach, leaped in the air and came down on it two-footed. Everything went white. The explosion echoed back and then Dabrowska was screaming.

Aker snapped his attention back to the immediate vicinity. There were demons everywhere. Dabrowska had been grabbed, she burst into flames, but even as she burned she pressed a Glock to the demon's head, firing again and again. It collapsed and the two of them were a bright conflagration, forever together.

James and Hardy were shoulder to shoulder, assault rifles roaring. Summers was beside Aker, down to his Glocks, but his accuracy was astounding. Double shots popped demon heads. At this range, 9mm could work it seemed. They lobbed the last grenades past the immediate threat in between shots, hoping to stem the tide of fiery death. Aker fired from the hip, taking more, then clicked empty with no mags left. Summers emptied a Glock and looked at Aker, shook his head. James's assault rifle dropped silent.

"Fall back!" Hardy yelled.

The fire was everywhere. Aker's skin seared, his fatigues blackening.

Stumbling backwards, fleeing the heat, Aker saw only two demons remained, almost on top of them. But they could outrun them, regroup.

Something hard hit his shoulder. Lost in the confusion and smoke, suddenly they were backed up into a corner. Somehow they'd got turned around.

"Which way is out?" James hollered.

"We've dead-ended ourselves," Hardy shouted, and his rifle clicked empty.

Aker stilled. This is it, he thought. Trapped, no ammo, no nothing. They'd used everything they had. They did okay, he supposed, got so close. He hoped there were others, somewhere, still surviving. Hardy and James hammered away with Glocks, but the two demons were still coming, the heat of them driving the survivors back against the wall.

Then Summers pulled a last grenade from his webbing. He'll kill us all, Aker thought. But at least we'll take them with us.

Summers gave him a wink, pulled the pin and ran forward, towards the last two bastards. The roar from his throat was bloodcurdling as he slammed an arm into each demon's chest, his momentum actually arresting their forward momentum briefly, then driving them back as he went up like a firework. *Strong bastard!*

Hardy, James and Aker dove for the gap he'd made, then they were flying as the grenade went up. Aker's ears sang from the concussion, heat lapped over him in waves, shrapnel and debris fell like hot rain. Something stabbed painfully into his leg.

Slowly everything stilled but for the crackle and flicker of fire.

Aker rolled over, wincing against the sting of burns. Smoke filled the corridor, spiralling back towards the open doors behind them. Now they saw the way out. James was on his feet, pointing. "Fire extinguishers."

Aker followed his lead, wincing at the stabbing pain in his leg but refusing to look, blasting away with clouds of CO_2. It seemed so pointless. Eventually the heat died down, the smoke thinned. There were no more demons. Aker limped, blood staining the leg of his fatigues where the shrapnel had punched in. Hardy was covered in burns and blood, a wide gash in his cheek, another in his arm. James was in a similar state. *Just three of us left*, Aker thought.

They headed back to the corridor where it had all started. The breach in the wall had become blocked with thick piles of fallen masonry. *Good old Gray, poor kid.*

"Think there are more behind there?" James asked.

Hardy shrugged. "No idea. They're contained for now at least. But let's hope that was all of them."

One lab door *thunked* unlocked and creaked open, a terrified face peering out. The demon corpses were nothing but melted glass and scorch marks, filling the corridor between them.

"Is it over?" the man asked, a strong Scottish accent.

"For now," Hardy said, voice heavy.

The man's red-bearded face split in a grin and the door rattled as he pulled it wide. He stepped back and let them in. The lab was big, all kinds of equipment Aker didn't recognise on shining steel benches. The red-haired man was tall. Two others were with him, a large man with a bald head and goatee beard, and a woman with black hair hanging in ringlets past her shoulders. "I'm John McLeod," the Scotsman said. "This is Ted Braun and Mandy Spelling. You lost a few back there, huh?"

Hardy nodded. "I'm Colonel Samuel Hardy. Corporal Aker and Private James. We need to fix ourselves."

He pushed McLeod aside and sat at a steel table. James and Aker joined him, pulled out medkits, helped each other where they could. The debris in Aker's leg had scored a deep cut into his thigh and he ground his teeth as James pulled it free and did some expert field stitching. There was silence until they'd finished and then McLeod stepped forward, nervously offering bottles of water. The three survivors grabbed them and swallowed greedily. There wasn't a part of Aker that didn't hurt, but it was nothing compared to his thirst. They downed three bottles each.

Eventually Hardy took a deep breath, looked up at McLeod. "And what are you doing here? Why were you locked in?"

"We're astronomers, Colonel, not soldiers. When the demons came, we were told to lock ourselves in and hide quietly. We did, but then we were trapped."

"Lucky for you."

McLeod smiled sheepishly. "We could have held out a few days, maybe a couple of weeks, but there's not much food and water here. You saved our lives. Thank you."

"Astronomers?" Aker asked. "On an army base? Why?"

McLeod grinned. "You haven't heard? No, of course you haven't. Classified intel and all that. Even you lot aren't in on it."

"In on what?"

"John," Ted Braun said in a low voice, like a warning.

McLeod waved a hand. "Don't worry about it, these people are our friends." He turned to face his colleague.

Braun frowned, then nodded, looked to the ground. Was he masking a smile? This trio of weirdoes was why they came all this way? Why all those good people died? Aker didn't like the situation at all.

McLeod turned back to Hardy. "We're not fighters, obviously. We're scientists. And we're so close."

"To what? Fixing the planet?"

"Understanding, Colonel!" The astronomer turned to a table behind him, large papers and printouts scattered all across it. "Look here."

They hauled themselves up, gathered around. Aker sensed a surge of hope through Hardy and James, like there may be a way out of this nightmare after all. But he was cynical. McLeod had said understanding, not recourse.

"It's taken some serious calculations, and we've lost communication with other scientists now, so it's hard to confirm anything else, but I know the truth. These ruptures in the planet, they're each the result of a meteor striking the earth's surface."

Aker barked a laugh. "Don't be ridiculous! Meteors big enough to cause those ruptures would be visible, like fiery rain. Besides, there's footage of some ruptures spontaneously splitting open, no impacts."

McLeod wagged an index finger, grinning. "Yes, yes, of course. But you misunderstand me. The ruptures are not caused by the meteor strike itself. The strike happens, the meteor is relatively tiny, it gets embedded in the earth, and then it... grows, like a planted seed. The size and timing of the ruptures opening is determined by the depth of the original strike, which is what made it so hard to recognise the pattern. The meteors themselves are so small they punch through the crust mostly unnoticed, but once in the ground, they cause a reaction that melts rock and earth. When enough magma has developed, the surface simply collapses into it, and boom! A rupture appears. Some long, some more round or irregular in shape, all dependent on the substrate into which they fall. And incidentally, this is why our communications failed. As the meteors increased in frequency, they began to destroy satellites as they passed. They pierced right through. Our orbital assets are space junk now."

Hardy leaned forward, brow creased. "This is some wild speculation, doc. And what about the fucking demons? Are you forgetting that hell is bursting up from below?"

"Not at all. They're not demons."

"Then what are they?"

McLeod pursed his lips. "When I knew the truth, I was silenced to avoid public panic and shipped out to a secure facility. The government studied my data, tried to determine if I was a crank or if I had something. Of course, during their deliberations the ruptures began opening faster and faster, everything turned to mayhem, and all order was lost, but I'd been at work a long time by then." McLeod turned a benign face to Braun and Spelling. "These two stuck with me. After all, the world was ending. We had to do something, and we figured it out. Look, I won't bore you with details. The short version is this: a meteor hits, it drills into the crust and starts to create magma, once enough magma is pooled, the meteor breaks apart releasing… eggs is maybe the best word. Those eggs roast in the magma as the pool grows. Eventually the eggs hatch and these glassy creatures emerge, swimming in the molten rock, growing bigger and bigger. The ground surface finally collapses into the rupture and, when they're strong enough, the creatures climb out."

"You studied all this?" Hardy demanded.

McLeod grinned. "I know it from my dreams."

"What?"

"You think they're aliens?" Aker couldn't keep the incredulity from his voice. Although he preferred this theory to the demon one, as it allowed his irreligiosity to remain intact.

McLeod laughed, raised his palms. "I suppose that's as good a description as any."

Hardy stepped back, shaking his head. "All this is ridiculous. Why are they just killing everyone? Is it an invasion?"

McLeod's eyes glittered. "A preparation!"

An alarm sounded, red lights flashing above a door at the back of the lab. Tension tightened through the group.

"Don't worry!" McLeod's voice was urgent. "It's not a threat. It's ready, that's all."

He hurried away, heading for the far door. The others followed, but one of the astronomers, Spelling, put a hand out to stop Aker. Once the others had moved away, she whispered, "It's not safe. You should leave."

"What's not safe?" Aker was disturbed by her slightly manic grin. There was genuine fear in her eyes, but also a kind of pity and more than a touch of madness.

"McLeod is…"

"Come along!" McLeod boomed, striding back towards them. He cast a searing glare at Spelling, then hauled on

Aker's arm, pulling him to catch up with the others. "You'll love this!"

Aker looked back. *What was she going to tell me?* But she was tight-lipped, staring at the floor as she hurried behind.

Blast doors at the back opened out into a vast room. The walls grey steel, reinforced, the ceiling high, criss-crossed with support beams, a gargantuan warehouse. It had to be at least three hundred metres long, maybe two hundred wide. At the back of the base, pressed up against the foothills of the mountains, it hadn't been on any of the maps or plans they'd seen. Hardy, Summers, and Aker had sat down only a few days before and confirmed their route to the base, and this was not marked as part of it. A huge circular construction sat in the centre of the room, easily a hundred metres in diameter. The air above it shimmered.

"The hell is this?" Hardy demanded.

McLeod grinned, that touch of madness in Spelling's eyes echoed across his face in magnitude. "It's our beacon!"

"Too late to run now!" Spelling said, laughing wildly.

The doors behind them hissed and slammed shut. James turned to hammer at the metal, looking left and right for a control to open them, but the walls were bare.

Braun smirked too, eyeing each of the three, sizing them up. He held a remote for them to see, to show how he he'd closed the doors. "You're here to share in the moment of glory!"

The alarm still buzzed, red lights all around the huge circular construction flashed. Aker ground his teeth, the three of them against three science nerds? No contest. Time to take control. Hardy strode for McLeod, murder in his eyes, when the Scotsman swept up a pistol. Hardy paused.

"You really are here to share our glory," McLeod said. "You should be honoured. You'll be the first!"

"The first what?" Hardy growled.

"Witnesses! Come and see!"

McLeod led the way to the giant steel ring. It had steps up the side at intervals, pipes and cabling snaked all around it. They climbed to the top, about three metres above the ground, and Aker's stomach fell away at the sight before him.

The circle was like a giant bowl and it contained galaxies. Like a lens out into deep space, he felt as though he could step off the edge and fall through infinity. Not an image, but some kind of portal. Cold emanated from it. Stars wheeled slowly by, spirals of glittering dust and suns, with utter, endless darkness in between. He grabbed for the rail, the only thing that stopped vertigo tipping him in. Hardy and James held on too, mouths wide, staring.

No wonder McLeod, Braun, and Spelling were insane, if they'd spent any length of time staring into this contained abyss.

"The fuck is it?" Hardy asked.

"Our beacon," McLeod repeated. "I learned how to make it from His instructions, in my dreams."

"You didn't build this in a couple of weeks."

McLeod laughed, his thick beard flapping. "No, of course not. You've got me. This is where it began. His voice came to me, searching, and I answered. He told me to build something to guide Him. Then He sent the meteor shower to clear the way, folded space to deliver His fire to cleanse all. We've known it was coming for months. I assured the government I could build something that would help us deal with the incoming storm, but I built this. They never suspected a thing, thought I was helping to contain the threat, when all along it was to attract Him."

"Who the fuck is him?" Aker asked, but Hardy and James had already followed the Scotsman's gaze.

Aker looked too, trying to see what had their attention so rapt. And then he picked it out, among the myriad stars and glittering nebulas. His brain stuttered. A writhing mass of tentacles, glistening glossy black against the matt darkness of space. Gargantuan eyes flickered open and closed among the thrashing multitude and he was in no doubt that it was moving inexorably closer. It had to be the size of a planet, or a sun, enormous beyond comprehension.

"What does it want?" Aker managed.

"Want?" McLeod asked. "Chaos. He sees life and civilisation and wants nothing more than catastrophe. Order offends Him."

"And you invited it here?" Hardy was aghast.

"I heard the magnitude of His whisperings through the void. I thought I was mad, but I was right. It wasn't my imagination. And I worked for years to attract His attention."

"Fuck, why?"

"For the glory of His gaze!"

One man's insanity had doomed the world.

"How long until it gets here?" Aker asked, trying to sound sane. "And how many more meteors and demons in the meantime."

"How long?" McLeod laughed. "Now! He's here now! That's why the alarms sound."

Aker pointed at the giant bowl. "Isn't that a projection of deep space? Light years away?"

"Yes, yes, but what is space and time to elder gods like Him? Imagine space is a sheet of paper and you want to get from one end to the other, what's the quickest way?"

"A straight line?"

"No! Fold the paper over and punch right through!" McLeod's laughter became manic and Spelling screamed.

Those unimaginably distant tentacles whipped up through the centre of the dish, bringing with them an icy stench of death.

McLeod danced. "He has noticed us at last! His fiery heralds have consumed enough life to wake His interest!"

"Too bad you won't see it," Hardy said. He snatched the pistol expertly from McLeod's hand, reversed it and fired.

McLeod's eyes went wide as the back of his head exploded and he toppled over the barrier to spin away. Vertigo swelled in Aker at the sight of him twisting downwards into infinity. Braun and Spelling turned to Hardy, both crouched low to fight, but both laughing like the lunatics they clearly were.

Hardy shook his head. "My fucking squad died for this shit?" Two sharp reports and both of them dropped. Spelling dead before she hit the deck, but Braun writhed and moaned. Aker snatched the remote off him and then kicked him roughly into the abyss, and James tipped Spelling's body to follow.

Reality began to collapse around them. Tendrils of what McLeod called an elder god were whipping about the huge space. But the space wasn't big enough to contain even a fraction of that being and actuality bent around them. The ceiling stretched miles up and flexed almost within touching distance at the same time. Aker's limbs felt crushed and pulled taut, his mind wax and jelly.

It's all too late.

Hardy pointed to the remote. "Come on," he said, his voice a million miles away and right in the shell of Aker's ear.

James staggered sideways and vomited. He stared at the glistening blackness writhing above and howled.

"Come on!" Hardy yelled, but James climbed onto the railing and dived in, gave himself to the god.

And why not?

Aker understood, began laughing manically. What was the point of any of it? Of anything?

Then Hardy snatched the remote and ran.

Stop him, a magnificent voice entreated, and Aker was only too willing to obey.

He ran after as the blast doors opened and Hardy barrelled through. Aker cried out as the stitches in his leg tore free, the muscle screamed in pain. The ground bent and undulated, he staggered and fell, got up and ran on. He grabbed his weapon as he passed it. The wound was agony and he used the pain to focus his attention, but Hardy easily outpaced him. He ran along corridors that seemed to never end and then suddenly found himself in bright sunshine. The building behind had swollen up, pulsing and breathing. Dozens of flaming demons swarmed about it. He saw the damage in the wall that Gray gave his life to close. Those glistening jet tendrils whipped from the curves of steel and simultaneously across the sky far above, separate and connected, immense, impossible. Clouds, purple and red, thick and cloying, pressed down on the planet as those giant god limbs flexed and waved among them.

Aker saw Hardy running into the munitions store, shouting, his words gibberish. Aker couldn't distinguish the Colonel's voice from the cajoling of the god all around. His leg screamed in agony, he staggered, unable to catch up.

Hardy smashed at the locks on the cage doors with a chunk of masonry, broke them off, and Aker realised what he was saying.

Nuke it nuke it nuke it

Nuke what? The beacon? Those bombs would level everything for miles, turn the entire region into a glass parking lot. Would that help? Was the god not already there, about to turn the world to gravel? But the thing was still in space too, bending reality.

Stop him...

The voice was everything, it was life and death. It hadn't finished manifesting? Travelling? Perhaps McLeod's beacon was a gateway the god needed.

Aker's god needed it!

But he was too far away to stop Hardy. Or was he?

He raised his weapon, grimacing at the weight, lined up his shot. As Hardy fumbled with the bomb arming mechanisms, hyper-real in the reticule, Aker squared the crosshairs on his Colonel's head and pulled the trigger.

click

Aker erupted into gales of laughter.

"No ammo!" he howled at the roiling sky. "No ammo! *HAHAHAHAHAHA!*"

The earth heaved, slick blackness whipped and writhed, the god cajoled, and Aker's mind snapped before he had any idea whether the god had arrived or the bomb detonated. Or if it even made a difference.

UNDER CALLIOPE'S SKIN

Originally published in SNAFU: Future Warfare, this story is my unashamed homage to all the great sci-fi horror/action flicks I've enjoyed.

Under Calliope's Skin

Andy Collins flicked his eyes to operate his virtual HUD. An adrenaline suppressant dumped into his bloodstream along with a tweak of endorphin as the Alliance Battlecruiser Belvedere fell out of jump with a bone-deep whine. He hated the inertia of re-entering real space.

"Take a moment to message your loved ones," Capstan barked. "We drop in three minutes."

The massive Lieutenant stomped from one end of the dropship to the other, enhanced musculature rippling under his form-fitting battlesuit. He paused at each team member to stare hard into their eyes, his virtual HUD relaying reams of data – pulse rate, blood pressure, serotonin levels, a hundred other markers. You couldn't hide a thing from a party Lieutenant. When he reached Collins, Capstan stared a moment longer.

"You okay, buttercup?" he asked, almost a whisper. His eyes were mean and his mouth pressed into a flat line as he waited for a response.

Collins watched the golden flicker across Capstan's eyeballs, wondered just what data he was reading. "Fine," he said, pleased his voice was strong. "You know I hate interstellar."

Capstan nodded once, paused to read another roll of information. His deep forehead relaxed under a mat of salt and pepper hair shaved close. "Just as well you're such a good soldier. Makes up for your flaws."

He stalked away before Collins could respond, but Collins allowed himself a smile. Capstan always acted the hardass, but he was a father to the whole squad. Though no one would ever say so to his face. He might love them all, but he'd kick seven shades out of anyone who suggested he had emotions.

"We green, Daisy?" Capstan called out.

"Across the board." The dropship AI's voice was a soft, velvety feminine.

Capstan turned at the head of the bay and scanned the two rows of marines facing each other, four along one side, three the other.

"We are eight of the best," he said, smiling to reveal the chromed shine of replacement teeth. He could bite through steel with those and his jaw augments. "In fact, we are *the best* eight and that's why we get sent out to these asshole shitheaps on the edge to do things no other fool would do. But this one is pretty routine, right?"

Laughter rippled around the bay and Capstan grinned wider.

"Fuck yeah, ain't no such thing as routine if we're involved. So here's what we know, and it ain't much." He tapped at his wrist pad and a holographic cube sprang into life between the two rows of warriors. A small moon swelled into view, orbiting a massive gas giant. "This is Calliope," Capstan said. "Fourth moon of the third planet in the Arteeria system. Distant scans revealed huge deposits of allerinium beneath the crust, and you don't need me to tell you what lengths the Alliance will go to for interstellar jump fuel. So a remote unit was sent to build a habitat. Once the robots had finished, a scientific team of twenty specialists was sent in to survey. Results were good for about two months and then all communications ceased. This is the last transmission."

He tapped his pad again and the three-dimensional map switched to a recorded video. A face leaned close to the camera, sweat running down the brow from soaked hair. The man's mouth was stretched in a wide grimace and his teeth were stained.

"That blood in his mouth?" Aiko Hayashi asked, her eyes narrowed.

"Looks like it," Tanveer Malik said. He glanced at Hayashi with a smile. "But is it his or someone else's?"

She flicked him a sour look, shook her head. Collins smirked. Those two were about due their occasional hook-up. It was a good tension diffuser that otherwise saw them fighting.

The man continued to stare and grin at the camera.

"He gonna say anything?" Collins asked.

Capstan shut off the image. "Nope. He stands there like that, not moving, not even fucking blinking, for three hours and fourteen minutes."

"The fuck?" Kirsten Watts said quietly.

"The transmission ends with a power drop," the Lieutenant continued. "Remote connections confirm the power was only out for a few minutes. As far as anyone can tell, the whole operation is still green. Except now there's no response to hails and no cameras anywhere inside the station are working."

"So they're sending us in," Charlie Finlay said.

Capstan pointed one finger at the tall, burly marine. "That's right."

Finlay grinned, his teeth like Capstan's, even brighter against sun-tanned skin. Wisps of blond hair poked from under the front edge of his helmet, an affectation that never failed to annoy Collins. "Cool," Finlay said in a low growl.

Collins scanned his squad mates, all buzzing with the excitement of a job about to start. He buzzed along with them, always keen for action, though the image of that sweating, staring guy with blood on his teeth gave him pause. But what threat were scientists to this team?

Red lights flashed and a siren wailed. "Ten seconds," Daisy said calmly.

"Here we go, my flowers!" Capstan shouted as he jogged to his rack and strapped in.

The dropship detached and fell for Calliope. The display up front showed the battlecruiser disappearing away from them, then space folded around it as it jumped away to sit far from the gravitational pull of the system and await the hail to pick them up again. Collins dumped a little pick-me-up into his blood as Daisy guided them in.

Locked and docked," Daisy said. "Pressures equalised.

You're good to go."

"Keep the engines ticking," Capstan said. "In case we need to facilitate a quick exit."

"I'll be ready," the dropship replied.

The Lieutenant moved to the hatch. "Form up."

The squad unbuckled and arranged themselves. Capstan took the lead, flanked by Hayashi and Finlay. Behind them were Alex Lau and Malik, followed by Henna Sterns and Collins. Watts, the medic, brought up the rear.

"All comms to closed group," Capstan said. "Inter-squad hails only, and keep those to a minimum. Rebreathers on."

Full face masks slipped from their helmets and joined seamlessly to their battlesuits. As soon as the toughened flexiglass was down, Collins felt the familiar tightening of his fatigues, every tiny gap closing, contained tight against even the hint of microbial attack. The flex-armour plates in the super-tough fabric swelled and shifted into place, a form-fitting carapace with micro-gyro strength and movement assistance. He felt safe in the body-hugging outfit, the familiar weight of his pack, ammo and weapons pressing down on him, the air in his helmet lightly scented with ocean salt as it passed through the suit's filtration system.

"Move out!" Capstan barked.

The hatch irised open and they jogged into the docking corridor of the scientific station. Lights were on, everything appeared normal at first glance.

"Check the map," Capstan said, and floor plans of the station appeared to each of them at a virtual distance of about thirty centimetres along with the rest of their HUD data. Each squad member was marked by name and a glowing icon. "I'm taking Hayashi and Finlay to the location of the last transmission, which is the engineering and mech bay. At the end is a vehicle bay for EVAC, so we'll account for assets there too." He highlighted the area off to one side of the sprawling habitat.

"Big fucking place for twenty scientists," Lau said.

"They intended it to house a lot more once mining commenced," Capstan said. "So it's going to take a while to cover everything." He zoomed out. "Malik, Lau, you two head north and start checking each of the sleeping quarters and lounges." He blipped a collection of about two dozen rooms along the northern edge of the centre. "Report as you go. Then work your way back towards the Command and Control centre, where we'll all regroup." A central room blinked.

"*Hai*," Lau said and peeled off, Malik jogging alongside.

"Sterns, Collins and Watts, you three need to go west and search the labs." A collection of six large rooms flashed three times.

Without waiting for a reply, Capstan hustled away to the right, with Hayashi and Finlay on his heels. Collins turned to his companions. "Ladies, after you." He gestured to his left.

Watts laughed. "Fuck you, soldier."

"I'll take point," Sterns said. "You two can enjoy my ass as we go."

Collins grinned. He most certainly would. And so would Watts for that matter. Though bonds throughout their squad were tighter than family, it was Henna who touched him most deeply, and he knew he was not alone. Sterns was a little bit mother and a little bit lover to most of them. And probably the most deadly when shit went down.

Watts nudged him with her rifle butt. "Wipe the grin off and focus, dickwad."

Collins winked at her. "I'll bring up the rear."

"Sure you will."

They moved forward, heavy assault rifles cradled ready, scanning as they went.

"It's too quiet," Sterns said.

"We know they're here somewhere," Collins said.

The corridor led to a large double door that hissed open as they approached. A lab lay beyond, all manner of survey equipment and data stations. Lights flashed, information rolled through holo-displays, everything looked normal. Except for the lack of surveyors. Collins approached one desk and leaned over to look at a coffee mug, still half full with black liquid. He blinked up his helmet scanner and it confirmed filter coffee, now long cold.

Watts gestured to a series of large tanks along one side.

"What the fuck are they doing in a mining survey station?"

"What are they?" Collins asked. Pale blue liquid rippled in each one, shimmering under bright lights embedded in the top. Each could easily fit three large men.

"Uterotanks," Watts said, eyebrows knitted. When the others gave her blank looks, she said, "Breeding tanks."

"For what?"

The medic shrugged. "No idea. But I've never seen them that big before."

"Well, doesn't that just bode all kinds of good," Sterns said. "Let's spread out, search the room."

They moved apart, helmet scanners processing reams of data as they let their eyes rove for anything that might be a clue.

"Here," Watts said. She pointed with the barrel of her weapon.

A chair was pushed out from under a desk, the seat and the floor around it smeared with blood. Scarlet drops sprayed across the desk and holo emitters. Watts stood back, hands raised as though framing up a photograph. They waited while she used her scans, then she said, "Best guess is a heavy blow to the back of the head, then another across the face." She mimed the actions, indicating the direction of blood spatter. "The victim fell here and was dragged a short way." The smears ended only a metre or so from the desk.

"Then what?" Sterns asked.

Watts shrugged.

"Picked up and carried off?" Collins suggested, his stomach tight.

"Maybe," Watts said. "But there's no more blood. Someone doesn't just stop bleeding when they're carried."

"Maybe they got wrapped up."

"Again here," Sterns said from across the room.

A similar pattern covered more equipment.

"When I was growing up," Sterns said, "my father used to tell this story about the draugen. It was an old-fashioned monster story, you know, a kind of Norwegian ghost or bogeyman. Bullshit designed to scare us. He used to say, 'Henna, if you don't behave, the draugen will come to get you!' I always thought that was an asshole way to make your kids do the right thing."

Collins had seen Henna take out an enemy squad single-handed while he was close to bleeding out. Then she had carried him back in. But in that moment he felt strangely protective of her.

"That's fucked up," Watts agreed. "But what's your point."

Sterns turned to face them with a grin. "I'm thinking maybe the bogeyman lives on Calliope, not Norway."

Collins was about to suggest they move on to the next lab when Sterns suddenly arched forward. A hole twenty centimetres across appeared in her chest, blood spraying forward as her ribs angled out like reaching bony fingers. She looked down in surprise, uttering a quiet, "Oh." The desk behind her was clearly visible through the hole, then she collapsed.

"The fuck?" Watts screamed, rushing over.

"Scan the fucking room!" Collins shouted. *Not Henna. No, no, no, not Henna!*

He crouched, moved in a circle looking for the source of the attack, but the lab was unchanged. There had been no muzzle flash, no sound. He quickly rewound the footage recorded in his HUD and watched again, playing close attention to Sterns. Nothing anywhere around her, then she launched forward, her chest exploded. *Oh*. She dropped.

Watts crouched beside the fallen marine shaking her head. "Dead before she hit the ground. Fuck. Henna!" As she rose to face Collins, she staggered to one side, then screamed as her left arm fell, sheared off at the shoulder. She sat down hard, blood arcing from the gaping wound. She scrambled for a patch can and frantically sprayed fast-expanding foam across the injury.

Collins began cycling through light bands. He swept his gaze left and right, looking through infra-red, microwave, gamma, ultraviolet, around and around, his vision a kaleidoscope of changing images, looking for anything that might be a source of the attack. Then movement. Subtle, almost immediately ceased. Without giving himself away, moving only his eyes, he looked back into the corner of the lab. Under the arm of some strange mechanism like a giant dentist's light, something stood stock still. Visible only in ultraviolet, it was a shape made of mirrors, quicksilver. No discernible features or details.

Collins raised his weapon and it came directly for him. Bigger than a man, it seemed to project itself forward on four pounding legs that thrust vertically up and down against the floor without a sound. Four more upper limbs stretched out, reaching for him, each ending in a long hand of three blade-like fingers. Its head was a flat wedge, arrowing forward.

Collins fired, his finger grinding against the trigger on full auto. The weapon barked deafening projectile death and gouts of fire, ripping into the creature. It staggered back, the wedge head splitting open as though it were screaming in agony, but still it made no sound. With less than five meters between them, Collins thumbed a mini-grenade from the barrel-mounted launcher and it exploded against the thing's torso, threw it back into the corner where it lay still. Collins staggered under the shockwave, but kept his feet.

"Lieutenant, everyone, we have aliens here!" he yelled over a squad-wide waveband. "Use ultraviolet!"

There was no reply. No blips marked their positions on HUD. He realised he hadn't seen their blips for a while. How long?

"Lieutenant?" Nothing. "Daisy?" Nothing. "Fuck." Collins hurried over to Watts, turning slow circles as he went, scanning everywhere.

"Make sure it's dead!" Watts said, waving him towards the creature he'd shot. Her face was pale and sweaty behind her visor, the slash of freckles across her nose standing out clearer than ever, but her shoulder was sealed up in med-foam. "I'm dumping painkillers like a junkie," she said. "I'm okay for now."

Collins nodded once. His eye fell on Sterns and he tore his gaze away, stifling a sob of grief and fury equally combined. Weapon trained on the inert thing in the corner, he approached cautiously. It seemed to flicker slightly, the mirrored body switching between invisibility and a dark, shining greenblack shell. "Cloaking device?" Collins whispered, as much to himself as to Watts. "And a sound suppressor?"

The thing's chitinous exoskeleton was revealed in the flickers to be split in several places by his bullets, a wider rent in the centre of its torso where the mini-grenade had exploded. Thick, black fluid leaked everywhere, presumably its equivalent of blood. The bladed fingers were extensions of its carapace, one or two of them spastically extending and retracting, a smaller many-tentacled hand-like appendage quivered under the shifting knives. It twitched and shivered, seeming to swell and collapse, its form fluid. It had no face to recognise, but a wide mouth in its wedge of a head and a thin, glistening line around the upper ridge that might have been some kind of visual organ.

It reached up weakly, blades flicking forward. Collins skipped back. Those things had gone right through Watts' armour and her shoulder. Right through Henna's body. He stepped back in, pressed the muzzle of his rifle to the band of maybe-eye, and fired a burst into its head. It danced and writhed under his attack and fell still. The flickering ceased and it lay there, a dark, ugly, armoured thing.

"Fuck you," he said and went back to Watts. He helped her up and she leaned on him heavily. "We can't leave Henna."

"We'll come back for her," Watts said. "The drugs are kicking in but I'll need your help for a minute. We gotta regroup."

"Stay on ultraviolet and be extra eyes for me."

She threw her arm over his shoulder and brandished her weapon. "I can still fire one-handed."

Collins glanced at the rifle so close to his head, nodded. "Just keep the muzzle up."

"Took my fucking arm," she said, voice low with incredulity. "Took Henna!"

"They'll build you a new arm once we get out. And everything here will die in Henna's name!"

He looked over at Sterns laying in a widening pool of blood as he led Watts away. "We'll avenge her," he said through gritted teeth, pushing away the emotion of the loss. He loved Sterns. They all did. She was the best of them.

"Three o'clock!" Watts yelled. She grunted as she swung her rifle up one-handed and triggered short, controlled bursts.

Collins winced against the volume of her rounds, kept his left arm around her waist to keep them moving, and matched her method with his right, as three mirror-bright shapes raced into the room from the lab next door. He pumped mini-grenades, drove them back. One broke right and tried to get behind them so he swung Watts and they danced a pirouetting retreat, raking fire and grenades as they went, ears ringing with the ordnance in the confined space. Smoke and light filled the room, equipment shards rained down. Lights blew out and sparks fell like bright orange snow.

They stumbled into the corridor and Collins spotted an emergency lock down beside the door and kicked it. His heel smashed through the glass covering and drove into the large button. Red lights flashed around the doorframe and a thick blast shield dropped as the double doors whooshed shut. Metallic thuds rang out as several masses hit the other side. The same three, unstopped by their bullets and grenades, or a new wave he couldn't know. And he didn't have time to care.

"Let's hope that holds them for now."

"There are other ways around," Watts said breathlessly.

"Let's just get to the C and C."

They ran for the Command and Control Centre, Collins calling for Capstan and Daisy the whole way, but comms remained dead. As the C and C drew within about fifty metres on their HUD map Capstan's voice boomed out. "...asses in here now, we're locking down in thirty seconds."

"We're ten seconds away," Collins yelled.

Something smashed and clattered behind them, then a symphonic rain of shattered glass. Watts tipped her weapon upside down on her right shoulder, let loose random short bursts, strafing left and right. Collins glanced back to see two glimmering masses, wider and lower than before, galloping up behind them, less than ten metres away.

The command centre came up on their left and he threw Watts forward. "Run!"

Spinning in place, he plucked a concussion shield from his belt and slammed it into the ground only a couple of metres from his feet, way too close for safety. As it pulsed into life, filling the corridor, he was lifted and thrown back, vision crossing like he'd been punched in the jaw. The creatures bounced back the other way.

Collins crashed hard against the C and C doorframe and fell inside. Capstan was at a control desk and punched a console. Heavy blast doors slammed closed and Collins lay face down on the hard floor, gasping. He looked up to see Capstan spare one narrow-eyed second for Watts' foamed shoulder stump, then return his attention to the console.

Hayashi stood beside the Lieutenant, Finlay nowhere to be seen. Of the four doorways leading into the C and C, only one remained open.

"Hey Aiko," Collins said, knowing better than to talk to Capstan at this point. "Finlay?"

She sniffed, shook her head almost imperceptibly. "He's in about six pieces back there. He just fucking split apart right in front of us. Henna?"

"Same thing."

"Fuck me, man." Hayashi looked back towards Watts. "Looks like you got too close as well."

"Looks like I got lucky," Watts said. "Finlay and Sterns! Shit. We've all been through too much together to lose two in a day. This ain't fair."

"When is it ever fair?" Capstan said. "And brace yourselves, because we're still two more down. Get over here and cover this door."

The four of them stood in a line in front of the only opening, weapons levelled. A corridor led away for about thirty metres before ending in another closed double door. Several rooms to either side were also shut. Watts insisted she was fine but Collins scanned her vitals, saw that she was surviving on drugs and grim determination. She badly needed to go under and set reknitters to work.

"Malik, Lau, respond!" Capstan said. The only answer was static hiss. "Seems like all comms are suppressed beyond about fifty metres. I can't tell how. Internal interference."

"They have to be coming, right?" Collins said.

Capstan gestured with his weapon. "Speculating is for fucking stock brokers. Watch and respond."

"Did you see them?" Collins asked.

Hayashi nodded. "Powerful cloaks, light and sound. Only UV works."

"You think the cloaks are tech or biological."

"Who knows."

"What do you think they are?"

She turned cold eyes to him for a moment. "Death."

Collins swallowed. He'd seen fear in Aiko's eyes and that made his stomach icy. He'd never seen her afraid of anything, didn't think she could be afraid. He dialled a cocktail into his bloodstream to calm his nerves, sharpen his senses, boost his muscles. Limits and safe doses be damned, he needed every advantage he could get.

"...incoming, Lieutenant! Fucking loads of them!" Lau's voice burst into their comms. "Can you fucking hear me?"

"Roger, Lau, we hear you. Please repeat."

"I said there are invisible bastards coming after us, can only see 'em on UV. We'll need some heavy cover fire!"

"Keep coming," Capstan said calmly. "I've tagged the door on your map. You both run straight for it and do not veer left or right. We'll fire around you. Collins, Hayashi, either side of the corridor, halfway up."

"Right."

Collins ran, Hayashi right beside him, and they dropped into alcoves for cover. Bursts of gunfire and explosions echoed along with Lau's voice screaming obscenities and promises of death and dismemberment, muffled by the double doors ahead. Lau and Malik's blips pinged onto the HUDs, closing rapidly.

"Here we go," Capstan said, and triggered the far doors to open.

Sound burst into full volume, Lau pumping bullets and mini-grenades blindly back over his shoulder as he ran, dragging the inert form of Malik with one hand. Blood smeared the floor where Malik passed.

Collins and Hayashi began setting blasts of cover fire. They both pulled larger explosives from their webbing and lobbed bombs over Lau's head. The corridor behind exploded into fire and smoke and resonating metallic screeches, and then Lau was through. Capstan slammed the far doors shut.

As booming reverberated from the other side, Collins and Hayashi dragged Lau and Malik into the C and C and Capstan sealed those doors too.

"Locking down!" he yelled.

A siren bleated, red lights flashed and blast shields slammed over the last portal. The siren stopped and everything sank into a submarine silence, even the compressors fell quiet as air recyc shut off. After a second or two, a new hum arose as the C and C went into defence mode, recycling its own air, providing all life support from inside the room, sealing itself off completely from the rest of the habitat.

Watts hurried over to Malik's prone form and crouched, wincing in pain, close to unconsciousness. She sat immediately back on her heels, deflated. Collins knew the others were seeing what he saw in his HUD. Malik's life signs were flat.

Lau put both hands on his head and turned in a slow circle. "Fuck, fuck, fuck!" He stopped suddenly, looked around. "Henna? Charlie?"

Watts shook her head.

"Fuuuuck!"

Watts tipped Malik half over to reveal his back open from right shoulder to left buttock. Stark white knobs of spine and a glistening half-orb of kidney showed through the blood and sliced flesh. With a grunt, almost a sob, she let him fall back.

Capstan crouched beside her. "How bad is it?"

She glanced at the mass of hardened foam covering her left shoulder. "Took it clean off. Got it covered pretty quick and I'm up to the eyeballs with antibiotics and painkillers."

"Okay. I want you to lie over there, put yourself under to reknit. We're gonna need to fight our way back to Daisy and I need you fit if not whole."

"If I go under, I'm out for half an hour."

"I know how it fucking works, soldier. We're safe in here. Go!" He turned to gaze at each of the survivors. "This room is in full bio-chem lock down and shielded. Let's take stock."

They let their masks up and removed helmets, stretched stiff necks. Capstan turned back to Watts. "Go!"

She ran her remaining hand through her short red hair and nodded, moved to lay down under a desk unit. Collins went with her, made sure she was comfortable.

"I'll monitor," he said.

She smiled. "Hold the fort. I'll be back in thirty."

"No problem. We got this." He put a hand against her cheek, his dark skin a shadow against her paler than ever alabaster. "Fix up."

He watched his HUD as she dialled in anaesthetic and her breathing settled to become deep and even. Nano reknitters in her blood, triggered awake by the anaesthetic release, immediately swarmed to any areas of hurt, rebuilding the flesh, sealing off wounds. Similar microscopics in her fatigues would already be doing the same to reseal her in where the sleeve had been sliced away.

Collins stroked a hand over her sweat-soaked hair once, then stood. "She's under," he said.

Lau was crouched over Malik, his forehead pressed to the dead man's brow. "I'm sorry, my brother," he whispered. As he rose, his eyes were wet, but murder lived in them.

Capstan flicked the map to front and centre of their HUDs. "Here's our way back to the dropship. Once Watts comes around, we go. Then we call in the cruiser, and flatten this shithole from orbit. Whatever those things are, they die here. We don't."

"Were there really loads of them?" Hayashi asked Lau.

He shrugged, mouth twisted in contrition. "Felt like it, but I don't know. I took out two, saw at least three more."

"You?" Capstan asked Collins.

"Took out one, and there were three after that. Hard to tell. Maybe two more. I think they were breeding the fuckers here."

"What?"

"The labs. It's not a mining operation."

Capstan nodded, lips pursed. "So what? Not our concern now. There's at least six to eight of the fuckers out there. Or maybe hundreds. And five of us. Doesn't matter. One door, three corridors, and we're back on the dropship and away, but we have to assume it's going to be a hell of fight to get there. You got thirty minutes. Check your gear and ammo."

Collins glanced at Watts, checked her vitals. They were already improving. Nano-reknit listed twenty six minutes to go. He reloaded his assault rifle and hers, double-checked his remaining grenades and other armaments. They were still well-equipped for a fight. To while away the time, he keyed up one of the consoles and started scanning through base logs.

"Incoming," Hayashi said quietly.

Their HUDs showed five lifesigns moving towards the C and C.

"Those things never showed up on our sensors before," Collins said. "Why now?"

"They're not life as our gear knows it," Hayashi said. "These must be something else."

"Cameras across the base are still out," Capstan said. "Sabotaged beyond repair. We'd need new circuit boards and bio-processors. Same with all the vehicles and base shuttles."

The lifesigns reached the western blast doors and there were three quick, sharp bangs. Pause. Three more.

"They fucking knocking now?" Lau asked.

"We assumed the scientists were all dead," Collins said. "But are they?"

Hayashi moved to the door. "What's the code for the view pane?" she asked.

Collins keyed up internal security and a moment later said, "Eight seven one hash D."

Hayashi tapped the code into a small pad on the door and a thirty centimetre square panel slid aside revealing a thick glass pane with a speaker grill below it. A small crowd of people outside slumped with relief.

"Please, let us in!" the front one said. His eyes were dark and haunted, his face blood-stained.

"How do we know you're safe?" Hayashi asked.

The scientists kept looking frantically behind themselves. "Please!" the front man repeated. "Some of our people went mad, homicidal, but we managed to hide. We're starving! We heard gunfire, knew rescue had finally arrived. Quickly, those monsters could be here even now. We can't see them!"

"And the ones who went mad?"

The scientist shrugged. "No idea!"

Hayashi turned to Capstan who returned her gaze with hard eyes. He ran his tongue along his top lip.

He lifted his chin to Hayashi. "Weapons up," he said quietly. Keeping his rifle level in one hand, he keyed the override with the other.

The door hissed open and five people fell inside, faces almost melting with relief. The door whooshed shut quickly behind them and Hayashi closed the view pane. The lead man strode towards Capstan with both hands out as though he were coming in for a hug. Two more men followed close behind and two women hung back.

"You're in charge?" the first asked. "Thank you! Thank you so much."

Capstan backed up, took a two-handed grip on his weapon. "Stay back!"

The front scientist shot forward, preternaturally fast, and fell on Capstan like a rabid dog. The Lieutenant squeezed a quick burst of fire, but the scientist wrapped him up like an octopus even as exit wounds exploded from his back. The following two joined the first, inhumanly quick and strong, slamming the Lieutenant to the ground. Capstan's weapon barked from inside the scrum and chunks of flesh and bone few out of the attackers, along with sprays of blood, but they continued their assault. Growling and hissing, snapping their teeth, hands rending in a blur.

Collins stepped forward and took line of sight to shoot

without hitting Capstan and squeezed off three quick headshots. As each skull exploded, that body fell still.

Collins dragged the corpses off the Lieutenant, but the man stayed down, blood-stained and twitching. His throat was a ragged mess, blood pulsing out across the floor. One eye was gone, his left cheek torn away from lips to ear, bite marks all over his face, head and shoulders, right through bone, exposing muscle and brains.

He'd given as good as he'd got with his enhanced teeth. The attackers lay around him with chunks missing. Silica filaments striated their exposed bones, glistened in their wet, red tissue. It glittered in their spilled blood.

Collins pulled a med-foam can from his webbing and stood numb, staring. Where the hell did he even start? There was more injury than flesh across Capstan's head, neck and shoulders. The Lieutenant gargled on his own blood, his remaining eye swivelled hectically in the socket. Collins sighed as Capstan's signs all flickered to a flat line.

The C and C was strangely quiet. He turned to see Hayashi and Lau, each with a weapon levelled at the two remaining scientists.

"Look in UV," Hayashi said.

The scientists stood as if frozen, not even blinking. Glass-like webbing criss-crossed their bodies like veins.

"Remember that last transmission?" Lau whispered.

"Poor bastards were already just puppets of those fuckers out there," Hayashi said. "We should have looked with UV before we let them in. Stupid."

Collins moved a little closer, weapon ready. Their eyes were as still as their bodies. "Fuck 'em," he said.

Hayashi and Lau fired simultaneously and the women slumped to the ground as their heads disintegrated.

"And then there were four," Hayashi said quietly.

Collins checked the medic's signs and was glad to see improvement rather than degradation. "Nineteen minutes until Watts is done."

Lau sat and triggered a holo-display, began working through comms diagnostics, trying to raise Daisy. "We need her hardware!" he said to no one in particular.

Collins returned to the console he'd been studying and continued to read. Eventually he found some encrypted logs and set about cracking them. It didn't take long with the military software on board his neural boost. "Motherfuckers."

"What?" Lau asked.

"This breeding program has been active for over nine years," Collins said, anger starting a hot flood in his gut. "According to this, surveys discovered previously unknown silicon-based lifeforms on this moon, most likely introduced hundreds of years ago."

"How long? By who?"

"It doesn't say. They live in warren-like structures in the first few metres of crust. Small, eight-limbed creatures that can reshape themselves and remould their exoskeleton. They naturally generate a tight energy field that interrupts light and sound waves, renders them silent and almost invisible.

"They were about the size of domestic cats, baseline intelligence roughly equivalent to a smart dog, no respiratory system to speak of, virtually no body heat, able to exist in vacuum and any temperature. They reshape their shells to carve through pretty much anything, including rock to make their homes, and consume silicate deposits in the crust to survive."

Lau shook his head, stared at the floor. "Fuck me. But those things are bigger than cats!"

Collins read on silently for a few moments, flicked between reports. "The fucking idiots started genetically manipulating them. They codenamed it Project: Future Warfare, began enhancing size and strength. They wanted to breed these things into trained warriors, invisible fucking killing machines under Alliance control."

"Shitheads!" Lau hissed.

"According to the most recent reports, they didn't understand the brain biology properly and the creatures' intelligence was exponentially enhanced along with size. They first began escaping confinement, then quickly developed a method to infect the humans and came back to gain control of the scientists. The last entry is from a Doctor

Alice Orszulok. She planned to go and sabotage all the vehicles so the things couldn't escape and then blow the place after transmitting this full report."

"She was successful in the vehicle sabotage," Lau said.

"They must have caught her before she did any more."

"But her message got through," Hayashi said.

They turned to her.

"What?" Collins asked.

"It's why we're here."

"Why didn't they warn us?" Collins asked. "Send more of us. We've got sentry cannons on the fucking dropship we could have deployed from the outset."

"Future warfare, remember." Hayashi shook her head, sighed.

"What?" Collins asked again.

"They wanted to watch us, see how their new soldiers perform. We're fucking fodder. But I don't think they realised the bastards had compromised all comms, base-wide and what we're carrying. We can't send a signal fifty metres, let alone back up to the Belvedere."

Silence fell over the room like a cold fog.

Lau punched a console. "Motherfuckers."

"When have we ever been anything but dispensable?" Hayashi said.

Collins caught a blip on another console and moved to check. It took him a moment to figure out what he was seeing. Then, "Hatches are opening and closing along the maintenance conduits. Several different locations, all leading towards the docking bay."

"Those things would never fit," Lau said. "People can barely squeeze along those fucking tubes."

Hayashi laughed derisively. "Reshape themselves and remould their exoskeleton."

"They're heading for the dropship!" Collins shouted. "We think we're hiding in here safe to regroup and they don't give a fuck. They're escaping."

"What do we do?" Lau asked.

"We have to stop them," Collins said.

Hayashi leaned back in her chair. "Why?"

"What?" Collins was starting to feel like an idiot, repeating the same word.

"They threw us to the fucking wolves. Or silicon shapechangers or whatever. So why do we care?"

"Two reasons," Collins said, anger rising again. "One, we're soldiers and we defend. Two, if they take our dropship, how the hell do we get home? You think Alliance will rescue us now we know this bullshit?"

Hayashi scowled.

Lau nodded. "He's right."

"Why are they in the conduits?" Collins asked.

Hayashi stood. "Because the only way to the docking bay is through here and we've sealed them out. They're bypassing. Let's go." She tapped at the console Capstan had been using and the southern door hissed open.

"What about Watts?"

"She's dead weight right now. We'll stop those fuckers first, then come back for her."

Collins downloaded the command codes to his neural implant. "Let's go."

The three of them resealed their suits and helmets and ran from the C and C, Collins remotely dropping the blast door behind them. *Hang tight, Watts,* he thought, then focussed all his attention on the imminent fight. Three corridors, two hundred metres, was all that stood between them and the dropship. He called out to the AI over comms. "Daisy, you hearing me?"

No response.

They ran on. Collins hailed Daisy again, still no response. They turned into the last corridor, maybe forty metres and one corner between them and the docking seal. "Daisy, you there?" Collins said.

"I'm here. I'm reading something in the conduits."

"Prepare to defend yourself," Collins said. "Deploy the sentry cann…"

The ground between them and the dock exploded upwards. UV clearly showed three glassy serpent-like creatures, three metres long, erupt up from the maintenance lines, tiny legs scrabbling at the broken floor. The squad skidded to a halt and backed up, firing controlled bursts, deafening in the confined space. As they pumped mini grenades, the creatures twisted and writhed like sentient smoke to evade the attacks. Bullets and explosions that did hit their targets had less effect than before.

"Their shells are flexible, must be thicker now!" Hayashi yelled. "They're adapting to our abilities."

"Marines, hit the deck," Daisy said over comms.

The three of them didn't pause, fell to their bellies. Three sentry cannons rolled around the corner and barked fifty-calibre destruction into the corridor. The sweeping fire ripped through the aliens and howled by just over the marine's heads, tearing the walls to shreds. The creatures fell in several pieces to the ground and silence sank over them.

Lau whooped and rose to his knees. "Way to go, Daisy!"

"I'm compromised," Daisy said in her calm, soft voice. "Get back to the C and C and lock down."

Lau frowned. "What?"

The sentry cannons roared again and Lau burst into a spray of blood and body parts.

"They've accessed my overrides from outside," Daisy said. "They're on the moon surface and gaining entry to me. I have no..." She fell silent.

"This was all a fucking distraction," Hayashi yelled. "Move!" She used elbows and knees to furiously snake her way back up the corridor.

Collins matched her as the sentry cannons swivelled towards them. He lobbed a concussion grenade behind as they went, the explosion knocking the cannons back. Their deadly stream of ordnance tore open the corridor ceiling and sparks flew as the lights went out. The cannons quickly reasserted their equilibrium and rolled on rubber tracks in pursuit.

Hayashi and Collins made the corner as more fifty cal fire ripped up the walls and floor behind them, and they bolted for the C and C. They fell inside, Collins triggered the blast doors which rang with cannon fire as they slammed down.

Laying on their backs, gasping, Collins and Hayashi

listened as the dropship powered up and launched.

Hayashi sighed. "Then there were three."

"With no hope of escape," Collins said.

He got up and checked Watts. Eleven minutes to go. He moved to the console and tried to key up a view, any view, to see what might be happening. None of the internal cameras were working, but an external array, watching the skies, was still operational. He tracked the dropship as it made orbit.

Space folded and the battlecruiser dropped out of jump, only a few hundred clicks from Daisy. Collins and Hayashi watched in silence. The dropship veered, heading straight for it.

"They recalled the Belvedere," Collins said. "You think they can gain control of a ship that size?"

Hayashi snorted. "Why not? They owned us since before we fucking landed."

"Reckon Alliance has any idea what's coming on board?" He sent repeated hails to the battlecruiser, knowing there would be no response. "I wonder how many of those bastards are on Daisy?" he said.

Hayashi shrugged. "Could be dozens. How many are still here? How big an army did those idiot scientists breed?"

Collins zoomed in on Daisy as she entered the Belvedere's docking bay. There were several moments of silence that seemed to drag into hours, then fire belched and billowed out into space as several hull panels around the bay split and buckled.

"Fuck," Collins whispered.

Nothing happened for several more minutes, Collins and Hayashi watched in silence.

Watts groaned and sat up, shifted her wounded shoulder. "We ready? Where's Capstan? And Lau?"

Shuttles began launching from the Belvedere, headed for the surface a couple of hundred clicks from the science station. Weapons ports opened along one flank of the battlecruiser and a wave of missiles launched, arcing down towards the habitat.

"Motherfuckers," Collins said.

Read more from Alan Baxter -
https://www.alanbaxteronline.com/my-books/

Acknowledgements

Huge thanks to A J Spedding and Matthew Summers, editors extraordinaire of the SNAFU series of anthologies, and to Geoff Brown, executive editor and publisher at Cohesion Press, for bringing these stories to light in the first place. It's been a pleasure to write for several volumes of the SNAFU series and I hope there are many more to come.

Story acknowledgements:

"In Vaulted Halls Entombed" – originally published in *SNAFU: Survival of the Fittest, Cohesion Press 2015*

"Raven's First Flight" – originally published in *SNAFU: Black Ops, Cohesion Press 2016*

"The Throat" – originally published in *SNAFU: Last Stand, Cohesion Press 2019*

"The Demon Locke" – originally published in *SNAFU: Medivac, Cohesion Press 2020*

"And Fire Poured Forth" – original to this collection, previously unpublished

"Under Calliope's Skin" – originally published in *SNAFU: Future Warfare, Cohesion Press 2016*

Devouring Dark

Finalist for the Aurealis Award, Ditmar Award, and Australian Shadows Award!

"Devouring Dark is a powerful tale of crime and death, cleverly crafted and flawlessly executed. I'm a fan of Alan Baxter and Devouring Dark is a perfect example of why. Do yourself a favor and join me for some shivers." – James A. Moore, author of *Seven Forges* .

Hidden City

"A grim and gritty fantasy noir with razor-sharp humor. I loved it!" – Tim Waggoner, author of TEETH OF THE SEA.

Steven Hines listened to the city and the city spoke. Cleveport told him she was sick. With his unnatural connection to her, that meant Hines was sick too.

Bound
Alex Caine #1

Finalist for the 2014 Ditmar Award for Best Novel!

Alex Caine, a fighter by trade, is drawn into a world he never knew existed — a world he wishes he'd never found.

The Roo

Something is wrong in the small outback town of Morgan Creek.

A farmer goes missing after a blue in the pub. A teenage couple fail to show up for work. When Patrick and Sheila McDonough investigate, they discover the missing persons list is growing. Before they realise what's happening, the residents of the remote town find themselves in a fight for their lives against a foe they would never have suspected. And the dry red earth will run with blood.

Manifest Recall

"If you like crime/noir horror hybrids do check out Alan Baxter's MANIFEST RECALL. It's a fast, gritty, mind-f*ck." – Paul Tremblay, author of A Head Full of Ghosts and The Cabin at the End of the World.

Following a psychotic break, Eli Carver finds himself on the run, behind the wheel of a car that's not his own, in the company of a terrified woman he doesn't know.

The Gulp

Strange things happen in The Gulp. The residents have grown used to it.

The isolated Australian harbour town of Gulpepper is not like other places. Some maps don't even show it. And only outsiders use the full name. Everyone who lives there calls it The Gulp. The place has a habit of swallowing people.
Five descents into darkness. Welcome to The Gulp, where nothing is as it seems.

Served Cold

2019 AUSTRALIAN SHADOWS AWARDS WINNER

16 provocative and intensely chilling tales blending horror, fantasy, and the weird.

"At turns creepy and visceral, Baxter delivers the horror goods." – Paul Tremblay, author of A Head Full of Ghosts and The Cabin at the End of the World

Crow Shine

Winner of the 2016 Australian Shadows Award for Best Collected Work; Finalist for the 2016 Aurealis Award for Best Collection; Finalist for the 2016 Ditmar Award for Best Collected Work.

"Alan Baxter is an accomplished storyteller who ably evokes magic and menace. Whether it's stories of ghost-liquor and soul-draining blues, night club magicians, sinister western pastoral landscapes, or a suburban suicide–Crow Shine has a mean bite."—Laird Barron, author of Swift to Chase.

The Book Club

Finalist for the 2017 Aurealis Award for Best Fantasy
Novella.
Honorable Mention, Best Horror of the Year, Vol. 10, ed. Ellen
Datlow.

Jason Wilkes's life takes a turn for the worse when his wife
fails to come home from her book club. Jason calls Kate's
'book buddy', Dave, who assures him she left hours ago.
Contacting the police, Jason finds them equal parts
sympathetic and suspicious. He tells them almost everything,
except that he's been hearing Kate's voice, calling as if from
far away. He certainly doesn't mention that he's seeing
shadows that reach for him.

Primordial
Sam Aston 1

"PRIMORDIAL has everything you'd want from a monster story—great characters, a remote location and a creature with bite!" – Jeremy Robinson,

Sometimes, the legends are true. When eccentric billionaire Ellis Holloway hires renegade marine biologist Sam Aston to investigate the legend of a monster in a remote Finnish lake, Aston envisions an easy paycheck and a chance to clear his gambling debts. But he gets much more. Something terrible lives beneath the dark waters of Lake Kaarme, and it's hungry.

Overlord
Sam Aston 2

What lurks beneath the ice?

Marine biologist Sam Aston is hired to explore a series of subterranean caverns deep beneath the Antarctic. Somewhere within this lost world of magnificent caverns and underground seas lies a source of limitless clean energy, but something guards this treasure. As enemies bent on obtaining this world-changing resource for themselves close in from above, Aston and his team plunge further into the depths, and discover they are not the first to come this way...and they are not alone.

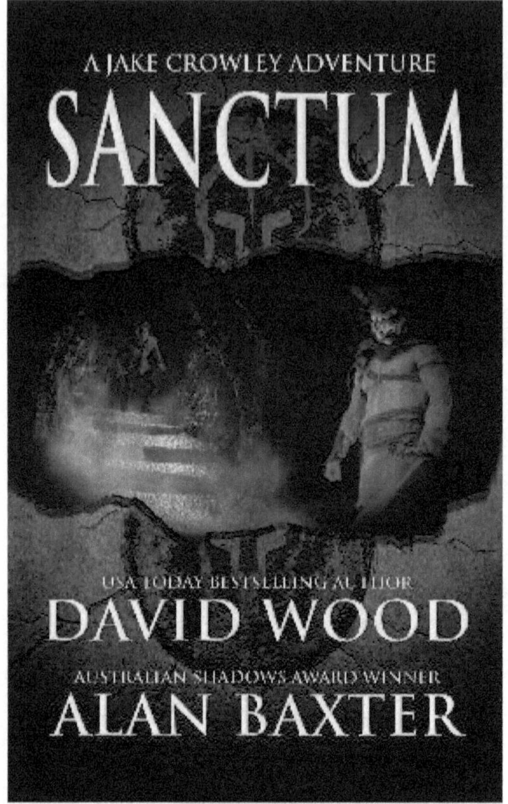

Sanctum
Jake Crowley Prequel

A quiet English village harbors a dark secret.

Trying to escape his past, veteran Jake Crowley takes a teaching position in the village of Market Scarston. But his slow rehabilitation is interrupted when a group of students are apparently attacked by Black Shuck, the legendary demon dog, and Crowley attracts the attention of a secret society dating back to the days of the Roman Empire.

Blood Codex
Jake Crowley 1

An ancient order. A deadly conspiracy. A race against time.
When Jake Crowley rescues Rose Black from assailants on
the streets of London, the two find themselves embroiled in a
mystery that could cost them their lives. People are dying,
and all the victims have one thing in common with Rose: a
birthmark in the shape of an eagle. From beneath the streets
of London, to castle dungeons, to the heart of Christendom
and beyond, Jake and Rose must race to stay alive as they
seek to unlock the secrets of the Blood Codex.

Anubis Key
Jake Crowley 2

Some doors should never be opened.

When Rose Black's sister goes missing, she once again calls upon Jake Crowley for help, but the two get more than they bargained for. The search takes them on a twisting journey, where danger lies at every turn. From ancient pyramids to lost cities, deadly cultists and conspirators lie in wait as Jake and Rose navigate depths few have dared on a pulse-pounding search for the ANUBIS KEY!

Revenant
Jake Crowley 3

Archaeologists excavating a mass grave in a historic New York City cemetery make a gruesome discovery: stacked like cordwood are skeletal remains going back decades, but all have one thing in common. Each skull bears a hole in the exact same location. When their friend is murdered investigating this bizarre discovery, Jake Crowley and Rose Black set off in search of the killer. Their path will take them to abandoned hospitals, hidden chambers, and into the depths of the strange world that lies beneath New York City in search of Edgar Allan Poe's secret journal

RealmShift
The Balance 1

Isiah is having a tough time. The Devil is making his job very difficult.

Samuel Harrigan is a murdering lowlife. He used ancient blood magic to escape a deal with the Devil and now he's on the trail of a crystal skull that he believes will complete his efforts to evade Lucifer. But Lucifer wants Samuel's soul for eternity and refuses to wait a second longer for it. Isiah needs Samuel to keep looking for the crystal skull, so he has to protect Sam and keep the Devil at bay. Not for Samuel's sake, but for all of humanity.

MageSign
The Balance 2

Three years have passed since Isiah's run in with Samuel Harrigan and the Devil. He has some time on his hands – a perfect opportunity to track down the evil Sorcerer, Harrigan's mentor. It should have been a simple enough task, but the Sorcerer has more followers than Isiah ever imagined, and a plan bigger than anyone could have dreamed.

With the help of some powerful new friends Isiah desperately tries to track down the Sorcerer and his cult of blood before they manage to change the world forever.

Dark Rite

A small mountain town hides a dark secret…

When the death of his father brings Grant Shipman to the tiny Appalachian town of Wallen's Gap, he believes his biggest problem will be dealing with the slow pace and odd townsfolk. But something sinister is at work. A dark power rises, an echo of the town's bloody past. A book of blood magic offers an unspeakable horror a gateway into the world of the living, and only Grant stands in the way of their Dark Rite.

About Alan

Alan Baxter is a British-Australian multi-award-winning author of horror, supernatural thrillers, and dark fantasy. He's also a martial arts expert, a whisky-soaked swear monkey, and dog lover. He creates dark, weird stories among dairy paddocks on the beautiful south coast of NSW, Australia. The author of more than twenty books including novels, novellas, and two short story collections, so far, you can find him online at www.alanbaxter.com.au or find him on Twitter @AlanBaxter and Facebook. Feel free to tell him what you think. About anything.

www.ingramcontent.com/pod-product-compliance
Lightning Source LLC
Chambersburg PA
CBHW021157110726
47900CB00002B/619